SHOCKED!

Eight feet away, a pronounced pout creasing her cherry-red mouth, was the girl. She vented a short hiss of annoyance and turned to the fence once more.

"You'll be killed," Havoc cried, on his hands and knees, and made a helpless gesture toward her.

An instinctive reaction prompted Blade to rise in an attempt to prevent the child from touching the lethal enclosure.

Glaring at them both, the girl sneered and pressed her flat palms against the links. A sharp crackling ensued and brilliant sparks of electricity danced about her fingers. She arched her back, her lips drawing back to reveal her neat, white teeth. For five seconds her entire body trembled.

Blade had to grab Havoc to stop the man from lunging at her. He watched in amazement as the trembling subsided and the girl suddenly threw back her head and cackled. A ripple coursed up and down his spine at what she did next.

The child started climbing the fence!

Other books in the *Blade* series:

#1: FIRST STRIKE
#2: OUTLANDS STRIKE
#3: VAMPIRE STRIKE
#4: PIPELINE STRIKE
#5: PIRATE STRIKE
#6: CRUSHER STRIKE
#7: TERROR STRIKE
#8: DEVIL STRIKE
#9: L.A. STRIKE
#10: DEAD ZONE STRIKE
#11: QUEST STRIKE
#12: DEATH MASTER STRIKE

DAVID ROBBINS

LEISURE BOOKS   NEW YORK CITY

**Dedicated to
Judy, Joshua, and Shane.
And to those who can.**

A LEISURE BOOK®

July 1991

Published by

Dorchester Publishing Co., Inc.
276 Fifth Avenue
New York, NY 10001

Copyright© 1991 by David L. Robbins

All rights reserved. No part of this book may be reproduced or transmitted in any form or by any electronic or mechanical means, including photocopying, recording, or by any information storage and retrieval system, without the written permission of the Publisher, except where permitted by law.

The name "Leisure Books" and the stylized "L" with design are trademarks of Dorchester Publishing Co., Inc.

Printed in the United States of America.

PROLOGUE

He had the craving again.

A full moon hung over the bustling city of Los Angeles. Many of the towering skyscrapers glinted in the pale moonlight, man-made monoliths rearing like mountains over the concrete valleys far below. A stiff, salty breeze off Santa Monica Bay stirred the otherwise sluggish air.

His heightened senses registered the sights, sounds, and scents of the night more acutely than those of any human. A quickening of his pulse signified his body was primed, his glands ready to release the chemicals. He came to an alley and paused to look both ways.

There were few pedestrians on the side street, and none were paying the slightest attention to him. Why should they? To them he appeared perfectly normal. How were they to know the truth?

Grinning in anticipation, he entered the alley and went into the deepest shadows. His body tingled, on the verge. But for a bit he hesitated, knowing he would be violating orders. Damn them all to hell anyway! How dare they make such an impossible stipulation?

The thought brought a fleeting moment of concern. He

knew damn well how they dared do it. In the century since the Great War, or World War Three as the ignorant survivors in America referred to Armageddon, no one had ever successfully defied them. They were who they were and they did as they pleased, and paltry mortals, hybrids, mutants, and his kind had better obey them or else.

Well, this time they had gone too far.

This time they had miscalculated.

The drugs were only marginally effective. They inhibited the craving, but not indefinitely, and he had been in the Free State of California for slightly over a year. Now it was early November! No wonder he couldn't fight the irresistible urge any longer.

He leaned against the wall, closed his eyes, and mentally kicked his glands into high gear, feeling the rush of potent chemicals surge through his veins. Caught in the grip of sheer ecstasy, he trembled in delight and almost forgot to direct the transformation. He'd done that once, a decade ago in Mongolia, and wound up as a formless mound of flesh. Thank God the brain remained intact no matter what other changes took place.

So what should he be? Speed was of the essence. He must satisfy the craving, revert, and get back before anyone realized he'd gone. What would be best in a city of humans? The obvious occurred to him and he chuckled.

A hooker would be ideal.

He opened the pores in his skin and let the chemicals seep out, saturating his clothes, rendering the fabric mutable. Unfortunately, prolonged exposure to air rendered the chemicals unstable after two or three hours. He would be stuck with whatever syle he was wearing at that time unless he treated the clothing again.

His head started to elongate, his facial features shifting. The prickling sensation in his lips and chest tickled. He wanted to giggle but suppressed the inclination. If a human discovered him now, while he was helpless, he might well be killed. Humans were incapable of understanding the change; they tended to view his kind with utter horror.

Both his arms and legs extended several inches and became much slimmer. The skin responded superbly to his every desire, flowing and shifting like a thing alive.

A minute went by. Then two.

He felt his fingers taper outward and the nails grow an inch in a second. His face acquired an oval cast. A wave of hair sprouted from his head and flowed to his narrowing shoulders. The sweet scent of the chemicals exuded by his body during the transformation tingled his nostrils. It had been so long since the last time that he almost slipped into a rapturous delirium.

At last the alterations were completed. Straightening, he blinked and looked down at the lacy red dress barely covering his shapely figure. Going female always gave him a creepy feeling; he'd much rather assume masculine guises, but in this instance the drastic change was prudent. He knew females of his kind who were equally reluctant to become males. It had something to do with natural biological imperatives according to the other ones he'd talked to.

He waited for the chemicals to dry and his skin to give off a human scent before venturing to the alley mouth. Checking to make certain no humans were nearby, he stepped out and turned to the left. He wished he had access to a mirror. Every part seemed to be in its proper place but accidents had been known to happen, such as the time Gorf had transformed and wound up with an extra leg. Which proved that a brief lapse of concentration could have humorous and potentially dangerous results.

Two teens approached, both devouring him with their eyes.

Good, he reflected, smiling. Everything must be in

order. He swayed past them, tempted but not foolhardy. A single mark was preferable.

At the next artery, Olympic Boulevard, he took a left and blended in with the flow of humanity. Even at such a late hour, almost midnight, the sidewalks were packed with people. He regarded all this fresh meat with amusement. Los Angeles was one of the few major cities to still be relatively intact, and it throbbed with activity twenty-four hours of the day. True, L.A. couldn't compare with Hong Kong or Peking, but it was still like one giant smorgasbord; all shapes, sizes, and age groups were present, making his mouth water.

He went several blocks, scanning the humans for a particularly choice morsel, when the unexpected transpired. Stopping at a curb to wait for the light to change, he was surprised when a hand fell on his right shoulder and someone spun him around.

"Hey, sister. What's happening?"

The speaker was a tall black man wearing an expensive brown suit. A gold watch adorned his left wrist and three gold rings decorated fingers.

"May I help you?"

Chuckling, the man placed his hands on his hips. "Ain't you the polite bitch? Yeah, you can help me by telling me what you're doing strutting your stuff on *my* turf?"

"I beg your pardon?" he said, and almost resisted when the man grabbed his right wrist and pulled him over in front of a closed music store, out of the way of the pedestrians.

"Don't play games with me, lady. Malcolm Luther isn't a guy you can take lightly."

Now what was all this about? he wondered, and decided to hold off teaching the human manners until he ascertained the reason for the man's behavior. "I wouldn't dream of taking you lightly," he said, "but I honestly don't know why you are so upset."

"You don't, huh?" Malcolm responded skeptically. "Then you must be new in L.A."

"How did you guess?"

"Easy. No one is dumb enough to cross me unless they don't know no better." Malcolm gestured along the block. "All the babes who work this district do so under me. It's mine, understand? And I get twenty percent of your nightly take. Hold out and you're a dead woman."

Now he understood. "Oh. You're a pimp."

The simple statement provoked Malcolm. He lowered his voice and hissed, "Don't ever call me that again. I like to think of myself as a merchandiser of sensual delights."

"An onion by any other name," he paraphrased, and felt Luther's hand close onto his right arm.

"You're coming with me."

"Where to?"

Luther didn't bother to answer. He headed toward a white limousine with tinted windows parked ten feet away at the curb. A man wearing black leather clothing stood beside the car holding the rear door open.

"Get in, bitch," Luther commanded.

Keenly aware of the few stares being directed in their direction, and not wanting to create a disturbance that would attract the police, he complied, restraining his temper for the time being. Sliding over to the opposite door, he primly folded his hands in his lap.

In came Luther, who waited until the other man shut the door, walked around the front of the car, and climbed in behind the wheel before getting down to cases.

"Okay, woman. No one treats me with disrespect. You're going to learn the hard way not to mouth off to me."

"I'd rather not."

The driver laughed.

"You don't have no say in the matter," Luther said, balling his right hand into a fist. "And who knows? After I'm done we'll go to my place. If I like you I may take you into my stable."

"I'd rather eat puke."

"What?" Luther responded angrily.

He saw no reason to delay. The tinted windows prevented anyone outside from observing the interior. Snaking both hands outward in a blurred motion, he took the men simultaneously, his left hand clamping on the driver's neck while his right seized the pimp's throat.

Both men reacted predictably. They grabbed at his wrists and tried to tear his hands loose. The fools had no idea what they were dealing with, and even if they had, there was nothing they could have done to prevent the inevitable.

He smiled sweetly and squeezed, feeling their necks burst like rotten melons, their flesh parting as his fingers pressed inexorably together, gore and blood dripping down his forearms.

The pimp and the bodyguard thrashed for a few seconds, the pimp blubbering and soiling his fine suit. Then they went limp and sagged.

So much for big, bad Malcolm Luther. He smirked, let go of them, and wiped his hands and arms clean on the pimp's jacket. Humming, he climbed out and walked to the sidewalk. No one paid any attention to him. The humans, as ever, were simpleminded sheep.

He resumed hunting, sashaying along Olympic until he reached Crenshaw Boulevard, where he turned right. Several drivers honked at him. He simply kept walking, confident sooner or later one of them would pull over.

Not a minute later a portly, balding man in a red sports car zipped to a stop and called out the open passenger window. "Hey, honey. I've got a grand here that says we can have the time of our lives."

Moving to the car, he leaned on the window and sized up his prospective supper. The guy was easily fifty or sixty pounds overweight, more than enough for a hearty meal. "You sure you can handle the action?"

Portly Butt laughed and slapped the seat beside him. "Why don't you climb in and find out for yourself."

"Don't mind if I do," he said, and deliberately sat next to the door instead of close to the driver.

The man accelerated and patted the seat again. "There's no need for you to be shy."

"I haven't seen your green yet, handsome."

Chuckling, the driver produced a thick wad of bills. "Is this enough for you?"

"More than enough," he responded, pleased that his vocal cords were performing so well. After using the same voice for over a year he'd been afraid that he might not be able to manipulate his pitch and resonance as adroitly as before. His concern had been groundless.

"Then why don't you slide on over here and we can start some serious cuddling?"

He made a pretense of gazing out the windows. "I don't want the cops to see us."

"Been picked up once or twice, huh?"

"Yeah."

"No problem. I'm staying at the Royale. Why don't we go there and get down and dirty?" the man asked, and smiled wickedly.

"I'm all yours."

The man beamed, and drove the seven miles to the Royale in record time. He braked near the entrance, and hurried around to open the passenger door as a valet came toward the car.

"Want me to park it for you, Mr. Webster?"

"Yes, son, I do," Webster responded.

As gracefully as possible, Webster's passenger slid out and stood, bestowing a friendly look at the valet. He really didn't care who saw him. The police, after all, would want to question a supposedly glamorous female suspect. Never in a million years would anyone regard him with suspicion once he resumed his current assigned guise.

"Hello, ma'am," the valet said huskily.

"Hi, cutie," he said, giving the boy a thrill. He let Portly Butt take his arm and escort him to the elevator. Thankfully, an elderly couple rode up with them and his supper kept his eager paws to himself.

The room turned out to be 504. Typical of the Royale, it was tastefully plush.

"Now we can get down to business," Portly Butt said happily after flicking on the light.

"Can't a girl have a drink first?" he asked.

"Sure thing, sweet cheeks." Portly Butt hurried to a small bar. "What would you like?"

"A Bloody Flesh."

"Never heard of it," Portly Butt said, looking over his shoulder. "Don't you mean a Bloody Mary?"

"No, handsome. Let me show you," he said, and walked slowly forward, restructuring the lower half of his face into its natural state as he did. He almost laughed at the horrified expression on Portly Butt's puss. Instead, he opened his mouth wide, exposing the triple rows of razor-tipped teeth lining his upper and lower jaws, and leaped, covering the ten feet in the single bound.

Portly Butt was parting his lips to scream when those jaws crunched down on his face.

CHAPTER ONE

The herculean giant sat in the back seat of the yellow taxi, directly behind the driver, immersed in deep thought. A black leather vest, fatigue pants, and combat boots clothed his seven-foot-tall frame, barely containing the bulging muscles that gave the illusion of being sculpted from solid bronze. Strapped around his waist were a matching pair of big Bowies, and resting across his stout thighs was a Marlin 45-70. Propped between his legs was an Uzi.

He absently stared out the window at the passing California scenery and brushed at the comma of dark hair that dangled down his brow. His gray eyes narrowed as he contemplated his impending homecoming. How should he handle the problem? he wondered. Before he could formulate a plan, the driver interrupted his train of thought.

"I can't believe it's *you*," the young man said. "I mean, no one is going to believe I had the head of the Freedom Force in my cab."

"Why not?" asked the giant.

"Are you kidding, Blade?" the awed cabbie said. "You're the most famous guy in California. My buddies are bound to think I made the whole thing up."

Blade said nothing. Such unwarranted flattering had been directed his way several times in recent months and he found it oddly discomfiting. True, he was the head of the Force, the elite tactical squad organized to protect the interests of the Freedom Federation, but in his estimation such a position hardly deserved the adulation heaped on him by the public.

Thinking about the Federation brought to mind the seven factions of which it was composed and how they might react to the upcoming confrontation.

Of all the factions, the Free State of California most resembled the California that existed over 106 years ago, prior to the Armageddon called World War Three. Thanks in great measure to its abundant natural resources, the postwar standard of living was higher in California than in any other area of the ravaged country. Even so, luxuries were confined to the privilege few and many citizens had a hard time acquiring the basic necessities. It had been the governor of the Free State who had initially proposed forming the Force, and then graciously offered to house the squad at a special facility situated outside Los Angeles.

The second most progressive faction, at least from a materialistic viewpoint, had to be the area of the Midwest and Rocky Mountain States now known as the Civilized Zone. The U.S. capital had been transferred to Denver during the war, and the former states of Kansas, Nebraska, Colorado, Wyoming, New Mexico, and Oklahoma and parts of Arizona and Texas had been incorporated into the new political entity.

By comparison, the remaining factions were much smaller both geographically and in population.

The Dakota Territory, once the states of North and South Dakota, was now controlled by the rugged horsemen called the Cavalry.

In Montana, the Flathead Indians had reclaimed the land originally inhabited by their remote ancestors and were now free of the white man's rule.

In northern Minnesota, in an underground city where their own ancestors had taken refuge over a century ago, dwelt the Moles.

Not all that far away in northwestern Minnesota, in the small town of Halma, lived refugees from the ruined Twin Cities who had adopted the collective name of the Clan.

And finally, the very smallest faction numerically but the one wielding the most influence in Federation councils, there was the Family. Also based in northwestern Minnesota, the group consisted of the descendants of a survivalist who still lived in the 30-acre compound he'd constructed prior to the ultimate folly. They would be the first to admit they owed their continued existence to the protection of their unique Warrior class, men and women trained to be fighters par excellence.

Blade thought about his fellow Warriors as the cab neared the Force HQ. He hadn't seen any of them—nor his beloved wife and son—for several weeks, ever since venturing into the arid, inhospitable Outlands of the Southwest.

"We're almost there," the driver announced.

The creature seated beside the giant yawned and declared, "About time."

Nodding in agreement, Blade glanced at his companion. "The others will be surprised to see you, Grizzly."

"I'll bet."

In prewar times those of limited understanding might have referred to Grizzly as a freak. The term he preferred, the term generally used to describe his kind, was hybrid. A genetically engineered mutation, bred by a demented scientist in a test tube in a laboratory, he had been endowed with a mixture of human and bestial traits. Like all hybrids, his animal traits were patterned after a specific species, in his case the terrible grizzly bear.

Grizzly stood over five feet eight, but enjoyed the physique of a powerhouse. A coat of light brown fur completely covered his body from head to toe. His torso, limbs, and shoulders were exceptionally thick, and a prominent hump existed between his shoulder blades. His face was decidedly bearlike; concave cheeks, elongated nostrils, a pointed chin, and a receding brow all added to the effect. The only article of approval he wore was a black loincloth.

"How do you feel about coming back?" Blade inquired.

"Nervous. If I had any brains I would have stayed in the Outlands," the hybrid said in his low, raspy voice.

"And miss your chance for revenge?"

Grizzly smiled, the expression devoid of all warmth. "Never. I want to carve the son of a bitch into bits and pieces."

The cab driver looked over his shoulder. "Do you mind if I ask who you guys are talking about?"

"Yes," Grizzly snapped.

Blade hardly noticed the fleeting terror that flickered across the driver's countenance. He was preoccupied with thoughts of two people he had cared for deeply, two people who were now dead. He must make certain their deaths had not been in vain.

Ahead appeared the electrified fence enclosing the Force Facility. Embracing 12 acres, the combination headquarters and training area included two concrete landing pads each 50 yards square for the VTOLs the Force utilized as primary transportation, plus hangars for the aircraft and, in the middle of the facility, three concrete bunkers. One was the supply bunker, another the barracks, and the third Blade's command bunker.

A pair of California Army troops were on guard duty

just inside the south gate. They stared suspiciously at the approaching cab, their M-16's in their hands.

"They won't shoot, will they?" the cabbie inquired nervously.

"No," Blade assured him. "The Force has had a few run-ins recently with certain gangs from L.A. Those men are simply being cautious."

A soldier sporting the two stripes of a corporal held his right arm aloft.

The driver braked and brought the vehicle alongside the closed gate.

Apparently unable to see inside because of the bright afternoon sunlight glinting off the windows, the corporal called out, "No civilians are permitted past this point. Who are you and what do you want?"

Blade opened his door and slid out.

Both guards gaped, then snapped to attention.

"Sorry, sir," the corporal blurted out. "We didn't know it was you."

"You've nothing to be sorry for," Blade replied. "You're performing your job properly and I'll be sure to mention your efficiency to your superiors."

"Yes, sir," the corporal said, grinning, and hastened to open the gate.

The Warrior leaned down to address the cabbie. "Will you wait here a minute? I need to get the money for the fare."

"You don't have it?" the driver answered, sounding stunned.

"Nope." Blade moved toward the gate and heard Grizzly's door open. Even if he hadn't, the shocked expressions on both soldiers would have told him the hybrid had emerged.

"Grizzly? Is that you?" the corporal declared.

"Do I know you?" the hybrid asked, joining the

Warrior at the entrance.

"You spoke to me once or twice back when you were on the first Force," the corporal said.

Grizzly studied the man for a moment. "Oh, yeah. Metz is the name, right?"

"Yes, sir," the corporal said, and added quickly, "We heard that you were dead."

"From who?"

"No one in particular. It's a rumor that's been going around."

The other trooper cleared his throat and looked at the warrior. "Excuse me for asking, sir, but didn't Captain Havoc go with you to the Outlands?"

"Yes," Blade confirmed, and scowled. "He gave his life in the line of duty."

"Uh-oh," the trooper said.

"What's wrong?" Blade asked.

Pointing toward the bunkers, the trooper said softly, "A younger brother of his showed up a couple of days ago to see him. When the brother found out the captain wasn't here, he got real upset. He's been staying in the barracks ever since."

"The barracks?"

"Yes, sir. I believe Doc Madsen gave him permission to sleep in Captain Havoc's bunk."

"I see," Blade said thoughtfully. So he wasn't back three minutes and already complications had developed. He didn't relish the prospect of breaking the bad news to the brother. "Thanks for the information."

The Warrior and the hybrid hiked toward the bunkers, passing the pair of gleaming VTOLs en route.

"Are you positive your new squad will accept me into their ranks?" Grizzly inquired, his tone betraying a rare uneasiness.

"Since when have you been concerned about what

others think?" Blade answered. "Don't worry about the new team. They're a great bunch to work with."

They covered ten yards in silence.

"I just thought of something else," Grizzly stated. "Which faction am I going to represent?"

"Pick one," Blade said flippantly although he'd previously pondered the same technicality. The Force consisted of a volunteer from each of the Federation members, with every recruit agreeing to serve for a period of one year, after which a replacement would be sent by the sponsoring faction. All members of the Federation were represented with the exception of California; Captain Havoc had been their volunteer and the governor would undoubtedly select someone of his own choosing to replace him. Leaving Grizzly in the cold, so to speak.

"I'm serious," the hybrid said.

Blade looked at him. "Since I'm the head of the Force and the Federation leaders gave me complete authority, I can select recruits as I see fit. If I want you on the team, you're on."

"Won't some of the leaders raise a stink?"

"Let them."

Grizzly scrutinized his friend carefully. "You've changed during the past year."

"Have I?"

"Yep. You're more of a hardass than you were before."

"I'll take that as a compliment," Blade said. He spied a cluster of people standing outside the command bunker and braced himself for the grilling that would take place. He intended to tell them the truth with one major exception, an exception he would deal with personally.

The hybrid, whose eyesight was keener than the giant's, said, "They've spotted us."

They certainly had.

A female voice whooped, "Blade! It's Blade!" Six

figures ran to meet the new arrivals.

Genuinely glad to see them, Blade beamed.

In the lead came the fleetest of the bunch, the volunteer from the Civilized Zone, a hybrid like Grizzly, a lean catman named Jaguarundi. He also had a coat of fur, only his happened to be reddish, and wore a black loincloth. As did the animal he resembled, his namesake, Jaguarundi possessed a small oval head, feline ears, eerie green eyes with vertical slits instead of circular pupils, and thin lips that were pulled back in a warm grin, in the process exposing his thin, tapered teeth.

Behind the hybrid came three people in a row.

On the left ran Raphaela, who hailed from the Moles. A beautiful redhead, she wore fatigues that almost matched the color of her eyes. Of all the new squad members, Raphaela had been the least experienced. But she learned fast and worked hard and had earned the honest respect of everyone else on the team.

Beside her was Sparrow Hawk. He was a Flathead Indian from Montana, and beaded buckskins covered his short but stocky five-foot-six form. His shoulder-length hair and eyes were both dark. On the left side of his belt hung a hunting knife. In his right hand he clasped a spear.

On the right jogged the volunteer from the Cavalry, an independent gunfighter called Doc Madsen. He dressed the part perfectly, wearing a black wide-brimmed hat, a black frock coat, black pants, and black boots. His shirt, however, was white. A gun belt slanted across his narrow hips, and in the brown leather holster on his right side rode a pearl-handled, nickel-plated Smith and Wesson Model 586 Distinguished Combat Magnum.

Bringing up the rear were two others.

One happened to be the recruit from the Clan, a husky black man whose name aptly fit his character: Lobo. He wore jeans, a blue shirt, a black leather jacket and knee-high black boots. His hair was styled in an Afro. He was about six feet tall, his 190 pounds almost all muscle.

The last man Blade didn't know, and he promptly reasoned it had to be Havoc's younger brother. He was surprised to discover the man in a Special Forces uniform, and detected the Havoc family resemblance in the young man's handsome, rugged features and striking blue eyes. This new Havoc had jet-black hair. Four stripes on his sleeves indicated his rank.

"You're back!" Raphaela cried in delight, halting in front of the giant and impulsively hugging him.

Blade couldn't return the favor because he had his hands full with the Marlin and the Uzi. He grinned and said, "Glad you missed me."

"Did we ever," Raphaela said, stepping back and blushing. Her gazed shifted to Grizzly, then looked toward the gate. "Where's Mike?"

The Special Forces sergeant stepped closer. "Yeah. Where *is* my brother?"

A shadow descended on the Warrior's face. He wished he could relay the news under better circumstances, but he had no choice. "Mike is dead," he informed them.

"No!" the younger Havoc cried in a flaring fit of commingled grief and rage. "No!" His face flushing crimson, he staggered backwards as if struck by a blow, then caught himself, glared at the giant, and charged.

CHAPTER TWO

The unforeseen assault took Blade unawares. Burdened as he was with the guns, he couldn't employ his hands to ward off the youth's rush without dropping them, which he refused to do. Instead, as the noncom grabbed at the front of his vest, he simply tried to dodge to the left.

Unable to check his momentum, the young Havoc ran into the giant's shins, tripped, and sprawled onto his stomach. In a flash he jumped up, still in the grip of his fury, and assumed a martial arts stance, the Kokutsu-tachi, most of his weight resting on his back leg with his front foot ready to flick out. "Not again!" he stated bitterly.

Grizzly moved between them. "Calm down, kid, before you hurt yourself."

"Kid!" Havoc exploded, launching a kick that would have caved in the hybrid's bearish face had it landed.

Only Grizzly was faster. He shifted, let the noncom's combat boot sweep past his ear, and grabbed the young man's leg. With a deft twist of his sturdy shoulders he sent the soldier flying.

Displaying remarkable athletic ability, Havoc landed on his shoulders and rolled to his feet in a smooth motion to assume another karate stance.

"That will be enough," Blade barked sternly while slinging both the Uzi and the Marlin over his shoulders to free his arms for action in case the order was ignored.

"Please, Steve," Raphaela intervened, moving up to the soldier. "Calm down."

"Calm down?" Havoc bellowed incredulously. "I just lost another brother!" Torment lined his face. He let his hands fall to his sides. "Not Mike too!" he declared, and repeated the statement in a whisper. "Not Mike too."

Blade couldn't blame the young man for being upset. During the tenure of the first Force yet another Havoc, another sergeant named James, had died in combat when the team took on savage pirates in the Canadian wilderness. Then James's older brother Mike had shown up to take his place. Now Mike was dead. That had to be some sort of perverse record; two members of the same family slain in a span of a year while serving in the same unit. "I'm truly sorry," Blade said softly. "I liked both of your brothers a lot. They were professionals in every sense of the word."

"Tell me about it," Steve Havoc said, making a discernible effort to compose his swirling emotions. "It's a Havoc family tradition. My father and grandfather were both career officers. "I . . ." he began, and broke off, overcome, bowing his head and closing his eyes.

"We understand," Raphaela said, putting an arm around his shoulders to comfort him. She led him off toward the woods located north of the bunkers.

For a while no one spoke. They merely watched the Molewoman talking softly to the distraught trooper until the pair halted at the tree line.

Lobo broke the silence. "I feel sort of sorry for the dude," he commented.

"As do I, my friend," Sparrow Hawk said. "Losing

loved ones grieves the soul."

"I don't know about that soul garbage. But I lost someone close to me once, wasted by lowlifes, and it sure ticked me off," Lobo said. "It taught me a great lesson, though. I learned not to waste time bawlin' my brains out." He smirked. "It's more fun to get even."

Doc Madsen was examining Grizzly critically. "Who is this?" he inquired.

"I know who it is," Jaguarundi stated, smiling. He stepped up and offered his right hand. "Hello, Grizzly. Long time no see."

"Hello, Jag," the bear-man said.

Blade was pleased that they knew each other. Both had been created by the vile Doktor; both had later rebelled against the madman and been imprisoned for their independence. After Blade had killed their creator they'd been eventually released to begin a new life. They tended to be loners by nature, and having a fellow hybrid on the team would make them feel more comfortable.

"There has been a rumor going around that you might be dead," Jag mentioned.

"I'd like to get my claws on the sucker spreading that rumor," Grizzly said.

Jag cocked his head to one side. "What happened to Athena Morris? I thought she went into the Outlands with Blade and Mike to find you."

"She did," Grizzly confirmed, averting his eyes. "She's dead too."

The others were deeply affected by the news. They'd met Athena before she departed, and her death on top of Captain Mike Havoc's dramatically underscored their individual mortality. They all knew she had served on the first team and grown to love Grizzly. Through the machinations of someone who wanted to destroy the Force, they had been driven apart. Grizzly had disappeared.

Later, when Blade received a report that Grizzly might actually be alive and staying at a town called Mesaville in Arizona, Athena had volunteered to go along. Blade broke the gloomy spell by asking, "Has General Gallagher phoned or been by?"

"Not in days," Doc Madsen answered.

"The only visitor we've had is the diaper case," Lobo added.

"Who?" Blade asked, and then understood. "I wouldn't call Havoc that to his face if I were you."

"Why not?" Lobo responded. "He's not in the same league as his older brothers. I doubt he could bust his way out of a soggy paper bag." He snickered. "Actually, the guy is a bit of a dork."

"Like you have room to talk," Jaguarundi remarked.

"Watch your mouth, Fur Face," Lobo warned. "I don't take kindly to being insulted by misfits."

Before anyone else could so much as blink, Grizzly moved, reaching the feisty Clansman in a single stride and gripping the front of Lobo's shirt in his brawny left hand. Hardly straining, Grizzly hoisted the black man into the air and held his right hand six inches from Lobo's eyes.

"Don't!" Blade exclaimed.

Grizzly made a rumbling noise deep in his chest and locked his fingers rigid and straight. Instantly, from under flaps of skin and fur located behind his fingernails and thumbnails, snapped out five-inch-long claws every bit as wicked as those on a real grizzly bear.

The Warrior took a half step, about to interfere, but changed his mind. Lobo knew better than to insult a hybrid—any hybrid. Most genetically engineered mutations had been grossly mistreated and reviled by humans during their lifetimes and were quite touchy about matters related to their creation. Jag had tolerated more verbal abuse from Lobo than Grizzly ever would, and it would be best of the Clansman became aware of the fact now; later he might learn the hard way.

His eyes the size of half-dollars when the claws popped out, Lobo swiftly recovered his composure and said indignantly, "Hey, let go of the threads, man. Clothes don't grow on trees, you know." He tried to pry the bear-man's fingers loose, but it was like trying to move iron spikes imbedded in concrete.

"Don't *ever* call either of us a misfit again," Grizzly admonished, his eyes blazing.

"Chill out, man," Lobo said. "I didn't mean to get your tootsies in an uproar. It just sort of slipped out."

"Then since I'm going to be around here for a while, I suggest you learn to keep your big mouth shut," Grizzly said sternly.

"You are?"

The hybrid abruptly let go, tumbling the Clansman to the turf. "Yeah. Blade asked me to join the Force again and I've accepted." He relaxed the fingers on his right hand and the claws immediately retracted.

Jaguarundi clapped the bear-man on the back. "You did? That's terrific news. I miss the company of my own kind."

Attempting to be dignified while on his butt on the ground, his chin arrogantly upraised, Lobo glanced at the Warrior. "Is this true?"

"Yes," Blade verified.

"Is he replacin' Mike?"

"No. He'll be an extra member."

"Didn't think we needed one," Lobo muttered, warily regarding the bear-man as he cautiously rose. "If we keep this up we'll be a full-scale army in no time."

"Not hardly," Blade said, moving toward his bunker. He paused to watch Doc Madsen and Sparrow Hawk introduce themselves to the new squad members. Now all he had to do was break the news to the Federation leaders and one other person. The thought hardened his features. That other person, none other than General Miles Gallagher, the liaison officer between the Force and Governor Melnick of California, had been systematically trying to destroy the unit for at least a year.

The Warrior turned and entered the HQ, walking down a flight of stairs to his office. Once inside, he flicked on the light, closed the door, and sat down behind the desk. Recent events unfolded before his mind's eye as he tried to sort out the pieces of the puzzle.

General Gallagher never had liked the idea of forming the Freedom Force. Almost two years ago, when Governor Melnick had first proposed the idea at a Federation summit meeting in Anaheim, the general had opposed it. Gallagher had claimed that California could take care of its own problems and didn't need to foot the bill for an unnecessary tactical team.

Blade had been surprised when the governor selected the general for the liaison post. He'd gone along with the appointment because neither Gallagher nor Melnick had a say in how the Force was run. As a precondition to becoming the head of the unit Blade had demanded complete authority and total autonomy. He'd figured he could prevent anyone from meddling in the squad's affairs.

Little had he known!

During the ten months the first Force worked together, Gallagher had reluctantly gone along with the program and been of marginal assistance. Not until after the Force took on the minions of the infamous Lords of Kismet in Alaska had Gallagher shown his true colors.

While Athena recuperated in a hospital from injuries she sustained, Gallagher had devised a clever ploy to seperate her from Grizzly. When other Force members died and Blade subsequently disbanded the unit, the general hadn't shed any tears.

But later Blade had decided to reform the team. Apparently, from the evidence he'd uncovered, Gallagher had then launched an intense, calculated campaign to discredit or destroy the Force. The list of underhanded tricks the general had used was as long as the Warrior's arm.

Gallagher had managed to embroil the Force in combat well before the team was ready. He'd arranged for them to enjoy a three-day pass in Los Angeles in the hope they would become rowdy, create an incident, and be blasted in the press. When he discovered Blade intended to locate Athena, he'd sent three drill instructors to break the giant into itty-bitty pieces.

But the worst of the general's offenses revolved around using Captain Mike Havoc as a spy. Havoc had revealed everything to Blade: how Gallagher had tried to convince the captain that the Warrior's negligence had resulted in Jim Havoc's death; how Gallagher had persuaded Mike to join the Force and gather any evidence of misconduct that could be used to discredit the giant; and how Gallagher had vowed to destroy the unit no matter what it took.

But why?

He'd been asking the same question ever since wrapping up business in Mesaville, and all he'd succeeded in doing was running in mental circles.

Now he had to decide how to confront Gallagher. Marching into the general's office and trying to force the man to confess would be pointless. Going to Governor Melnick was also out of the question because he needed proof, not hearsay. Maybe he could—

The telephone rang.

Annoyed by the distraction, Blade swept the receiver to his ear. "Hello?"

"Blade?"

VENGEANCE STRIKE

"Speaking."

"Oh. It doesn't sound like you, sir. This is Corporal Metz."

"Yes, Corporal. What can I do for you?"

"Nothing for me, sir, but that cab driver is still waiting for his fare. He's a bit ticked off and bugged me to remind you."

Blade didn't know whether to laugh or slap himself in the forehead. He'd forgotten all about the cab in his preoccupation with General Gallagher. "Tell him I'm on my way."

"Yes, sir."

The Warrior hung up and opened the top drawer, where a tin box rested in the right-hand corner. He took out two twenties, stuffed them in a pocket, and after depositing the Uzi and the rifle in his chair, hurried out.

Grizzly, Jag, Doc, Sparrow, and even Lobo were chatting amiably when Blade emerged from the bunker and sprinted to the south. They stopped conversing to stare at him as he went past.

"A problem?" Grizzly called out.

"The cab fare," Blade reminded him with a smile, and hurried to reach the gate.

Corporal Metz and the other soldiers were arguing with the driver, who stood just outside and closed the gate with the middle finger of his left hand flipped up to emphasize his side of the dispute. Metz turned and sighed in relief when the giant arrived.

"This turkey was threatening to climb over the fence if we didn't let him in to collect his dough. I told him the fence is electrified with enough juice to fry his buns to a crisp, so he tried to climb the gate and we had to shove him off."

Blade took the bills from his pocket. "You can relax," he told the driver. "I have your money."

"Took your sweet time about it," the cabbie complained. "I could have been halfway back to L.A. by now."

The Warrior nodded at Metz, who pulled the gate inward a yard so he could step out. "How much was the fare again?"

"Twenty-nine dollars and fifty cents," the cabbie stated crisply.

"Here's forty," Blade said. "Keep the change."

"Really? Thanks." The driver held the twenties up to his nose, as if sniffing to verify they were real, then grinned and pocketed them. "I wasn't worried. I knew a famous guy like you wouldn't stiff me."

Corporal Metz made a sound that resembled the snort of a bull elk.

Ignoring the trooper, the driver got into his cab, gunned the engine, gave a cheery wave to the giant, and departed.

Blade started to turn when he spied another vehicle rapidly approaching the compound, a green topless military jeep doing well over the posted speed limit. At the wheel sat the sole occupant, an officer sporting several rows of medals above his left jacket pocket, and as the jeep and the cab went by each other he glanced at the cabbie. Blade recognized the officer's profile and clenched his fists.

It was General Miles Gallagher.

CHAPTER THREE

Blade stood rooted in place, struggling to control his surging anger, as the jeep screeched to a stop directly in front of him.

The general looked through the windshield, thoughtfully studying the Warrior, then killed the engine and hopped out. A bulldog of a man with brown eyes and crew-cut brown hair, he smoothed his uniform jacket, adjusted his hat, and walked boldly forward. "Do you want to talk here or elsewhere?"

"I should break your neck right here and now," Blade said softly so the guards couldn't overhear.

"But you won't," Gallagher stated confidently. "You wouldn't murder an unarmed man in cold blood."

Blade's eyes narrowed, his voice tempered steel. "*Don't tempt me.*"

Gallagher blinked, glanced at the troopers, then indicated the road with a nod of his head. "Why don't we take a little stroll and clear the air?"

"Suits me just fine," Blade said. He walked on the general's right, his hands draped meaningfully on the hilts of his Bowies. A glance over his shoulder showed the guards eyeing them quizzically.

"I appreciate your notifying me to let me know you were back," Gallagher said sarcastically.

"How did you find out?" Blade asked. He suspected that the general had an informant at the Facility, perhaps one of the Regular Army troops who pulled the guard shifts. But even so, even if someone had phoned the officer the minute the cab arrived, there was no way Gallagher could have made the trip from L.A. to the site in such short time. So how had he done it?

A smug smirk creased the general's face. "I have my ways."

"You have your *nerve* showing up after the stunts you've pulled," Blade declared, resisting an urge to pound the man into the ground. He reminded himself that any unwarranted violence would land him in hot water with the Federation leaders. Everyone knew about his long-standing feud with Gallagher, and if he tore into the general without the proof needed to justify his actions, there would be some who claimed he'd acted out of personal bias and who would call his position with the Force into question. Gallagher was not without influential friends.

"I take it that Havoc has told you everything?"

"What do you think?"

Gallagher went several strides, his hands clasped behind his back, before answering. "Where *is* Mike, by the way?"

The query confirmed Blade's suspicion that a soldier had phoned the general. How else would Gallagher know that Havoc hadn't returned? "He died in Mesaville."

"Do tell," Gallagher said, turning his head away. His shoulders bounced slightly as if he was laughing inwardly at the news.

Blade halted. They were 20 yards from the gate, far enough that the troopers couldn't eavesdrop. "Look at me," he commanded.

Hesitating, Gallagher slowly complied, his face composed but his eyes twinkling. "I'm sorry to hear about Mike."

"Bull."

"Athena didn't come back either, did she?"

There was no sense in hiding the truth, Blade reasoned. The general would discover the facts eventually. "No."

"I see," Gallagher said, clearly pleased. "How sad."

His hands closing on the Bowies, Blade leaned toward the officer. "You're pushing me, you son of a bitch."

Gallagher pursed his lips and took a half step backwards. "I shouldn't do that, should I? Especially since you can't touch me now. With Havoc and Athena dead, there isn't anyone who will testify on your behalf if you try to press charges."

"You think you have it all figured out."

"Correct me if I'm wrong," Gallagher said, "but there isn't a damn thing you can do. Even though you believe you know the truth, you're powerless to take any action against me."

The sight of the general's mocking countenance proved more than Blade could take. His left hand flashed out and seized the front of Gallagher's jacket, and his rippling thighs bulged as he lifted the stocky man off the ground.

Surprisingly, Gallagher took it in stride, his expression resigned, his hands still clasped behind him.

Blade nearly punched the officer in the face. On the verge of swinging, he curbed the impulse. As much as he craved revenge for Gallagher's foul manipulation of the Force, he couldn't bring himself to do it. The general had been right about one thing: Blade wasn't the type to kill an unarmed man in cold blood or, for that matter, to slug an unresisting foe. Disappointed in himself, he relaxed his hand and let Gallagher drop.

Grinning in amusement, Gallagher held his footing and straightened. "I'm glad you got that out of your system. Maybe now we can discuss this situation like intelligent adults."

"We have nothing to discuss," Blade told him.

"Oh? You certainly can't expect us to continue on as if nothing had happened."

"No. I expect you to resign your post as liaison."

"That's not possible."

"Don't play games with me, Gallagher. You've tried your best to destroy the Force. Either quit or I'll demand that the governor give you the boot."

Gallagher chuckled. "You always have been too naive for your own good. Melnick and I are close friends. He won't fire me just to please you."

"We'll soon find out."

"Be sensible. Why don't you do the right thing and disband the Force? Then you can return to your wife and son at the Home and live happily ever after while the Free State of California gets by quite nicely without your pathetic services."

The Warrior folded his massive arms across his broad chest. "Which brings us back to square one. Why do you want the Force disbanded?"

"You already know."

Blade nodded. "You've made no secret of the fact you think the unit is unnecessary, but there has to be more to it than that. No one goes to all the trouble you have for so petty a reason."

"My reasons are my own," Gallagher declared. He made a show of checking his watch. "How time flies. I have a meeting with the governor in an hour so I'd better head back to Los Angeles."

"Just like that?"

The general chuckled. "Just like that. Unless you want

to kill me in front of those gate guards?" He began to walk toward the jeep. "Nice talking to you. We should have chats like this more often."

"It's too bad you're hurrying off," Blade said, at a loss to explain the officer's cocky attitude. True, from a strictly legal standpoint Gallagher hadn't committed any crimes, but he'd caused various members of the Force immeasurable grief. Oddly, the man acted as if he truly didn't care that Blade intended to make him pay for the sorrow he'd visited on the others.

"And why's that?" the general said over his left shoulder.

"There's someone at the Facility who would like a few words with you."

Gallagher kept walking. "Oh? Who?"

"Grizzly."

Halting so suddenly he came close to tripping over his own feet, Gallagher spun. "Grizzly?" he repeated, his tone tinged with a trace of apprehension.

Blade nodded, enjoying the man's uneasiness. "Do you mean to tell me that your spy didn't let you know the good news? Grizzly returned from Mesaville with me. I've reactivated him on the Force."

"You can't do that."

"It's already done."

"Which Federation faction is he representing?"

"None. Consider him a free-lance member."

Frowning, the general looked at the gate, then at the Warrior. "The leaders of the Federation will never go for this. Each faction is supposed to provide one volunteer, that's all. There was never any mention of free-lance personnel."

"I'll convince them it's a wise move," Blade said. "After all, Grizzly has more combat experience than most of the current members. He's a great asset to the team."

"I don't like it one bit."

"I don't blame you," Blade stated, smiling. "I know that I wouldn't want to be in your shoes."

"Meaning what?"

"Meaning Athena told Grizzly all about how you were responsible for convincing her to dump him. She made it plain that the whole scheme to fake her death was your idea. All the heartbreak they suffered was your fault."

General Gallagher rubbed his hands together.

"Grizzly plans to look you up real soon," Blade mentioned politely. "If you'll wait here, I'll go get him."

"Some other times perhaps," Gallagher said. He pivoted and took only a few steps before drawing up short at the sight of someone running in their direction.

Blade heard the drumming feet and looked, wishing it would be Grizzly and disappointed to see the young noncom, Sergeant Steve Havoc, instead. What did he want?

"General Gallagher," Havoc said, pounding to a halt and saluting smartly. "May I have a minute of your time, please?"

"Do I know you, soldier?" the officer replied.

"No, sir. I'm Staff Sergeant Stephen Havoc, Detachment A, 77th Special Forces Group."

"Havoc?" Gallagher said. "Are you any relation to Captain Mike Havoc and Sergeant James Havoc?"

"They were my older brothers, sir."

"How old are you, Sergeant?"

"Twenty, sir."

The general gestured at the Force Facility. "And what are you doing here?"

"I'm on leave, sir. I thought I would pay Mike a surprise visit, but when I arrived he'd already left for the Outlands," Havoc said, his voice close to breaking.

"I'm very sorry about your brother, son," Gallagher

lied. "He was a superb officer."

"Yes, sir."

"Well, if you'll excuse me," Gallagher said, beginning to walk off.

"Sir, I'd like to make a request," Havoc stated urgently.

"In regards to what, Sergeant?"

"Replacing my brother on the Force, sir."

Blade took a stride forward. "You don't want to rush into anything, Steve. Take a week and think it over."

"Nonsense," Gallagher said, glancing at the Warrior in the manner of a cunning wolf about to feast on a hapless sheep. "If this young man sincerely wants to be on the Force, he deserves fair consideration."

"Thank you, sir," Havoc gratefully declared.

"How long have you been in Special Forces?" the general inquired.

"Almost two years, sir."

"Seen any combat?"

"A few skirmishes with raiders along the southern border. That's about it, General."

"I see," Gallagher said, scratching his chin.

"I'm probably stepping way out of line," Havoc continued in a rush, "but I know you're the man who has the final say in picking California's volunteer for Force duty. And since I saw you with Blade as I was on my way out of the compound, I figured I'd take a gamble and ask that you put my name on the list of applicants." He paused. "It would mean a lot to me, sir, and to my family. The Havocs have served in the military for generations, and all with distinguished records. My brothers were killed while trying to fulfill California's obligation to the Federation. I'd like to take up where they left off and prove that a Havoc can do the job."

For fully 30 seconds Gallagher made no reply. Then he turned toward the Warrior again and winked before facing the eager noncom. "I won't bother placing your name on the list," he stated.

"Oh," Havoc said forlornly, his hopes dashed.

"Because as of this minute you *are* the new recruit representing our glorious State."

Havoc's mouth dropped. He beamed, forgot himself, and took hold of the general's hand to vigorously shake it. "Thank you, sir. Thank you. This is an undeserved honor. How will I ever repay your kindness?"

Chuckling, Gallagher pried his hand loose and patted the younger man on the shoulder. "I'm certain you'll find a way. And don't worry about the paperwork finalizing the transfer. I'll personally call the commander of the 77th Special Forces Group and inform him of your new status. He'll arrange for your personal effects to be sent immediately."

The noncom's face radiated profound gratitude. "Thank you again. I won't let you down. I swear it. I'll be the best damn volunteer on the squad."

"I bet you will," Gallagher said, and pointed at the Force Facility. "Why don't you go break the good news to the members of your new unit?"

"Yes, sir." Havoc saluted, spun, and raced off.

Blade waited until the young man was out of earshot before remarking, "I've got to hand it to you, bastard. You never miss a trick."

"Why, whatever are you talking about?" the general asked in feigned innocence.

"You know very well what I'm referring to. You've put a novice in a squad that should only have pros."

"I don't see what you're complaining about. This new Havoc is no greener than Raphaela, Lobo, or Sparrow Hawk," Gallagher noted. "Which isn't saying a whole hell of a lot." He laughed and hurried to his jeep.

Smoldering like a volcano, Blade stood at the side of

the road and watched the officer drive off. Every instinct told him he should have gutted Gallagher and been done with it. By trying to adhere to the letter of the law he'd left himself wide open for reprisals, and there could be no doubt that the general would try something soon.

But what?

CHAPTER FOUR

The Warrior discovered the answer the very next day. But first other events of significance occurred.

No sooner was he back at his desk in the command bunker than boots pounded on the stairs, and a moment later a rapid knock sounded on his door.

"It's unlocked."

In came a grinning Stephen Havoc. He marched up to the desk and saluted proudly. "Sir, I'd like to have a word with you if I may."

Leaning back in his chair, Blade rested his hands in front of him and scrutinized the newest member of the Force. Neither as big as Mike Havoc nor as muscular as Jim Havoc, this younger brother possessed traits reminiscent of both. He had Mike's intelligent blue eyes and Jim's square jaw. And there was no denying he had a powerful build, but it was a physique still in development, a body that hadn't yet been tested to the limits of its endurance and carried a few more spare ounces than would a superbly conditioned form. "What can I do for you, Sergeant?"

"I wanted to apologize for my behavior earlier. When I heard that Mike had died I just lost my head."

"Understandable," Blade said.

"He wrote me about you, you know."

"He did?"

"Yep. So did Jimmy. They both rated you as one of the best men they ever served under," Havoc disclosed. "Mike wanted me to meet you, which is part of the reason I came here on my leave."

The Warrior gazed at a small mirror on the opposite wall. Two brothers had respected him highly; two brothers were dead. What if the same fate awaited the third?

"I know I'm not anywhere near as skilled as Mike and Jimmy were," Steve stated. "But I'll give one hundred percent of myself. You can count on that."

Blade nodded, impressed by the man's eagerness and determination. "I'm sure you will."

"And I hope you'll forgive me for not going through proper channels to get this appointment, sir."

"There's nothing to forgive. I have no control over the recruitment process each faction follows."

Havoc smiled. "I won't let you down, Blade. I was serious about proving that the Havocs can cut it on the Force. Our family has always prided itself on sterling performance. I'll take up where my brothers left off and do our family name proud."

"Just don't get carried away with proving yourself," Blade cautioned. "If you do, you'll become careless, take needless risks, and in the process you could endanger the entire unit."

"I won't," Havoc vowed.

Blade pursed his lips, reflective for a bit. "Tell me a little about yourself, Steve."

"What would you like to know?"

"Anything."

Havoc shrugged. "There's not much to tell. I graduated from high school and went straight into the military, just like my father wanted. I—"

"What did *you* want to do?" Blade asked, interrupting.

"Sir?"

"Didn't you have any plans of your own?"

"The Havocs have always gone into the military after high school. It's traditional."

"I see. Go on."

"Well, I went through basic and managed to get accepted in Special Forces," Steve related, and honestly added, "My brothers pulled a few strings for me."

"You must have demonstrated ability in your own right or Special Forces would never have accepted you, brothers or no brothers."

"I suppose," Havoc said. "My black belt probably had something to do with it."

"In karate?"

"Yes, sir. I studied under the same sensei as Jimmy and Mike. Had my black belt by the time I was fourteen."

"How is your marksmanship?"

"I obtained my ribbon right out of basic."

The more Blade learned, the more pleased he became. Steve Havoc might be green, but he possessed great potential. Clinching the fact was Havoc's rank; only those demonstrating exceptional competence made staff sergeant in under two years. The last laugh might turn out to be on General Gallagher. He thought of another question he'd like to ask, but someone chose that moment to barrel down the steps with all the finesse of an inebriated elephant.

Lobo rushed into the office, breathing deeply from his exertion. "Blade! Come quick!"

"What is it?" the Warrior asked, rising.

"You've got to see for yourself," Lobo said, excitedly jabbing a finger at the doorway. "Hurry, Big Guy! The others are waitin' for you."

Perplexed, Blade ran up the stairs trailed by the

Clansman and Sergeant Havoc. He squinted in sunlight and searched for his people.

"This way," Lobo said, taking the lead and going around the corner of the bunker, bearing northward.

Blade had seldom seen the Clansman move so fast. He followed, and spied the rest of his unit grouped together within ten yards of the trees. The northern third of the Facility had been preserved in its natural state for training purposes, and dense woods and a few low hills extended from the bunkers to the north perimeter. "What's up?" he inquired as he joined them.

"We see her but we don't believe our own eyes," Jag said softly, pointing.

Looking to the northwest, Blade was astonished to behold a young girl of ten or twelve standing on a knoll 30 yards distance. "It can't be," he blurted out.

"I said the same thing, pardner," Doc Madsen stated.

The girl had curly blond hair with bangs that hung to her eyebrows. She wore a spotless white dress and bright red shoes. Smiling happily, she waved at them.

"Don't ask me where she came from," Raphaela commented. "One minute she wasn't there, the next she was."

"This is most mystifying," Sparrow observed.

Again the girl waved, beckoning them.

Blade shook off his astonishment. This couldn't be, he told himself, yet there the girl stood. She seemed oddly familiar in a bizarre sort of way.

"How the hell did she get there?" Grizzly wanted to know. "She couldn't have climbed over the electrified fence."

"Maybe there's a break in the fence somewhere," Raphaela speculated.

"But a break would register on the equipment at the guard shack," Grizzly reminded her. "The grunts would know about it and have it repaired in no time."

"Besides," Jag said, "our facility is way out in the middle of nowhere. What's a girl like that doing wandering around by herself in the wilderness?"

No one had an answer.

"What do we do?" Raphaela asked the giant.

"We go get her, what else?" Blade responded. He glanced at the hybrids. "Grizzly and Jag, you'll stay here. No offense, but she might be scared stiff and run off if you go any closer."

"We understand." Jag said.

"Humans," Grizzly muttered.

"Let's go," Blade said, and made for the knoll and the still-beckoning girl. He racked his brains in an effort to find the reason she seemed to be familiar, but failed.

"Move slowly," Raphaela suggested. "We don't want to frighten her."

The child took a few steps forward, then primly folded her hands at her waist and swayed from side to side.

"Weird little brat," Lobo remarked.

They advanced half the way and the girl simply swayed and grinned.

"Hello," Raphaela yelled.

The girl curtsied.

"She looks like she's tryin' to lay an egg," Lobo mentioned. "I never realized it before, but white kids sure are geekoids."

"What the dickens is a geekoid?" Doc Madsen asked.

"You know. A total nerd. A loser."

"How would you like to eat lead?"

"On the other hand," Lobo amended, "some white kids are downright def."

"Lots of lead," Doc said.

"Hey, that was a compliment, dude."

"Since when is making fun of folks who can't hear a compliment?"

Blade halted. "Quiet, both of you." It occurred to him that the child might be intimidated and flee if all of them drew closer. "Raphaela, why don't you go on ahead. She might feel more at ease."

Nodding, the Molewoman walked slowly nearer.

"Maybe some of us should flank the kid," Lobo proposed. "For all we know that could be Goldilocks and she might sic the three bears on us."

Sergeant Havoc sidled next to the Clansman. "Are you always this way?"

"What way?" Lobo asked.

"Always," Sparrow Hawk confirmed.

Blade hardly paid attention. The crack about Goldilocks had staggered him. Now he understood why he'd mistakenly thought he knew the girl; she resembled the drawings of Goldilocks in one of his son's books. It had to be coincidence, he rationalized.

Unexpectedly, the blond girl suddenly spun and ran over the crest, giggling in delight.

"What the hell," Lobo said.

Raphaela cast a questioning glance over her shoulder.

"After her," Blade ordered, and took off. "Fan out," he shouted at the others. "Don't let her get away."

"Shouldn't we go back for reinforcements?" Lobo queried.

The Force members rapidly covered the ground, Raphaela reaching the top of the knoll a dozen yards ahead of her companions. She stopped and peered intently at the vegetation below.

"Where did the child go?" Blade asked as he halted.

"I don't know," Raphaela said. "She disappeared."

Not so much as a leaf stirred in the forest. Not a speck of white showed among the weeds and undergrowth.

"This is gettin' spooky," Lobo stated.

"Look!" Sparrow Hawk exclaimed, pointing to the

northeast.

Blade did so and saw the girl a hundred hards off, leaning against the trunk of a towering tree. As before, she beckoned them onward.

"She couldn't have gotten that far in such a short time," Doc said.

"But she did," Sparrow stressed.

"I *really* think we should go for reinforcements," Lobo advised.

"Don't be ridiculous," Sergeant Havoc replied. "It's just a little girl, for crying out loud."

Blade jogged down the far side of the knoll. "We can't let her get away. Stay together." He wished now that he'd brought Jag along. The cat-man qualified as one of the fastest beings on two legs, and had once been clocked at doing over 50 miles an hour. The hybrid could catch her in no time.

Inexplicably, the blond girl paid no attention to the Force members and started dancing in a circle, spinning and leaping in balletic movements. She danced and danced until her would-be rescuers were less than 20 feet away. Then she laughed and skipped behind the tree trunk.

"We've got her now," Doc predicted.

They converged on the enormous tree, confident of success until they rounded the bole and found only more trees and brush before them.

"Where is the brat?" Lobo snapped, looking right and left.

"I don't know," Blade said, bewildered, and at last he admitted the truth to himself. Despite the testimony of his own eyes that they were chasing a dainty child, his combat-forged instincts told him otherwise. No normal child could do as this one was doing.

"What the hell is going on here?" Lobo wanted to know.

"Beats me," Doc said.

"She must be hiding close by," Raphaela stated.

"Guess again," Sergeant Havoc said, and motioned to the northeast.

Frowning, Blade swiveled and spied the blond sprite far off at the very edge of the Force compound, right beside the electrified fence, her hands behind her back as she skipped and jumped in juvenile abandon.

"Oh dear God," Raphaela breathed.

The girl waved at them, then faced the fence and seemed to be studying its metal links. Her right arm tentatively lifted toward the barrier, then lowered.

"If she touches it she'll be electrocuted," Raphaela said in alarm.

"I'll stop her," Havoc proposed, and raced ahead at full speed.

"Wait," Blade directed, but the young noncom kept going.

"Don't worry," Havoc called back. "I'll save her."

"What an idiot," Lobo said.

"Stop!" Blade ordered, realizing the soldier had no intention of complying and intuitively guessing that this was Havoc's way of proving himself, of demonstrating his competence to the others. Blade bounded in pursuit, his arms and legs flying, his strides twice the length of a typical runner's, his immensely strong physique serving him in good stead, enabling him to gradually overtake the new recruit. Unfortunately, he wasn't gaining quickly enough.

Havoc was fast, extremely fast, exhibiting the stamina and pacing of a seasoned long-distance runner. He shouted to the girl as he ran, "Don't touch the fence!" never breaking his rhythm.

"Stop!" Blade tried again without success. The young man possessed great potential, but he was more obstinate than both his brothers combined. And Blade had noticed that Steve, possibly because of his age and inexperience, wasn't the stickler for military protocol his brothers had been. Mike and Jim had rarely addressed the Warrior without capping their statements with a respectful "sir," yet Steve did so frequently. Not that it bothered Blade. He'd tried repeatedly to get the older brothers to lighten up, to relate to him on a first-name basis, and he'd do the same with the younger Havoc.

The girl had turned and was regarding the two men with an air of detached amusement. She twisted and reached for the fence again.

"No!" Havoc bellowed. "Don't!"

Pausing, the child looked at him, grinning impishly, her fingers inches from the deadly current surging through the metal links.

The Warrior drew within ten feet of Steve Havoc. He saw that the noncom would reach the girl before he could overhaul him, and a peculiar sense of dread filled his being, a feeling that he must stop Havoc at all costs or tragedy would result.

With an airy laugh the girl moved her hand a fraction nearer to the fence.

"No!" Havoc shouted again, still three yards from her, and launched himself forward, his arms extended.

Just as the girl skipped aside.

CHAPTER FIVE

Blade observed the noncom tense in preparation for the leap, and dived forward at the same instant Havoc did. His steely leg muscles, as superior to the soldier's as Havoc's were to a mere boy's, propelled him across the intervening gap in the twinkling. With his attention exclusively focused on the trooper, he only vaguely glimpsed the girl moving to the left.

Nothing stood between Havoc and the fence and he had no way of checking his momentum.

The Warrior's hands closed on the noncom's ankles in midair and he wrenched backwards, bringing both of them up short and causing them to tumble onto their sides on the hard ground, Havoc close enough to the fence to hear the voltage humming.

Blade released the soldier's boots and looked up. Eight feet away, a pronounced pout creasing her cherry-red mouth, was the girl. Her blue eyes blazed with a feral light. She vented a short hiss of annoyance and turned to the fence once more.

"You'll be killed," Havoc cried, on his hands and knees, and made a helpless gesture toward her.

An instinctive reaction prompted Blade to rise in an attempt to prevent the child from touching the lethal enclosure.

Havoc scrambled forward a few feet, than halted in stark horror.

Glaring at them both, the girl sneered and pressed her flat palms against the links. A sharp crackling ensued and brilliant sparks of electricity danced about her fingers. She arched her back, her lips drawing back to reveal her neat, white teeth. For five seconds her entire body trembled.

Blade had to grab Havoc to stop the man from lunging at her. He watched in amazement as the trembling subsided and the girl suddenly threw back her head and cackled. A ripple coursed up and down his spine at what she did next.

The child started climbing the fence!

In methodical movements, raising first one hand and then the other, the girl pulled herself even higher, not bothering to use her legs or feet at all. Bluish green light flickered in a macabre aura around her. She reached the metal bar at the top, halted, and seized a strand of the barbed wire that rimmed the fence.

Footsteps thudded on the earth as the other Force members arrived. Blade ignored them, unable to tear his gaze from the girl.

Drawing her knees onto the bar, the girl looked down at the Warrior and smiled. "We'll meet again," she said as sweetly as a saint, and forced two of the strands apart so she could slide through and drop to the ground beyond.

"Wait," Raphaela urged.

The girl didn't pay any attention. Pivoting, she pranced into the woods, moving due east this time. The vegetation closed behind her, and soon her white dress and golden locks were no longer visible.

VENGEANCE STRIKE

None of the startled witnesses to the incredible event spoke. They stared at the forest, collectively transfixed.

Predictably, the Clansman found his voice first. "Did you guys see what I saw?"

"Yes," Raphaela said.

"I don't know *what* I saw," Doc commented.

Blade straightened, hauling Havoc upright also. He stared at the fence and saw scorch marks on the metal links where the girl's flesh had touched the barrier.

"That sure as hell wasn't no kid," Lobo stated. "Nothin' human could do what she just did."

"I agree, my brother," Sparrow Hawk said. "That must have been a demon."

"Now don't start with that Great Spirit mumbo jumbo," Lobo responded. "There's got to be a logical explanation."

"Like what?" Sergeant Havoc asked.

"If I knew that, I'd set up a crystal ball in L.A., and make me a fortune," Lobo said, and chuckled.

Scanning the woods, Blade recalled her last words. "We'll meet again." She—or it—had been playing with them all along, leading them on, intentionally luring them to the fence. Perhaps she'd planned to slay one of them from the beginning. If he'd been a hair slower, she would have succeeded. Which reminded him. "Sergeant Havoc."

"Yeah?"

"Consider yourself on report until further notice."

"What?" the noncom exclaimed.

"You heard me," Blade said, pivoting on his heel and walking in the direction of the bunkers. Since it might be a while before the girl returned, there was no sense in hanging around waiting for her. He had a feeling she would pop up when they least expected.

The others followed, Havoc in the forefront.

"Let me get this straight, sir. You're putting me on report because I tried to save that little girl's life?"

"No, you're on report because when I give an order I expect it to be obeyed."

"But I didn't think—" Havoc began.

Blade glanced at him in stern disapproval. "No, you didn't. I told you to stop because I suspected something was drastically wrong. Had you listened, you wouldn't have put your life in danger."

"I thought I was doing the right thing."

"You were wrong."

Lobo laughed and clapped the noncom on the back. "Thanks, dude. You've made my day."

"How so?"

"It's great to have someone else in trouble for once," the Clansman said. "I'm glad you showed up. Now the Big Guy has someone else he can pick on besides me."

"Blade doesn't pick on you," Raphaela mentioned. "There are all kinds of reasons why you're always in hot water."

"Name one," Lobo said.

"Okay. You don't listen half the time. You never know when to keep your big mouth shut. You slack off during training sessions. You're always picking arguments with everyone else. You—"

"I said name *one*," Lobo reminded her testily.

Sparrow Hawk came alongside the Warrior. "With your permission I could circle around the outside of the fence and pick up the demon's trail. I might be able to track it to wherever it came from."

"Thanks for the offer, but no," Blade said.

"I would be careful."

"I'm sure you would. And if anyone can track that thing, you can. But until I learn more about it, I'm taking no chances. For all you know the girl could be waiting

VENGEANCE STRIKE   53

out there for some of us to show up."

The Flathead hefted his spear. "It would be her mistake."

Blade looked at him. "Sparrow, do you really believe the child is a demon?"

"Demon is the English word. But yes, my people do believe in good and bad spirits, in entities that bring blessings to humankind and in beings that bring harm."

"Have you ever seen any of these evil entities?"

"No. But the shaman of our tribe and others have encountered them. They are hideous and wicked beyond words. Long before the white man came to our land, they existed. And they will exist long after all of us are gone."

Although Blade seriously doubted they were up against a demon, he possessed tact enough not to say so to his friend. He'd fought his share of mutations, monsters, and bizarre creatures since becoming a Warrior and subsequently the head of the Force. He knew there must be a more mundane explanation.

But *what*?

That evening, while catching up on the mountain of paperwork that had collected on his desk while he was off in the Outlands, Blade heard someone descend the steps, and looked up to find Grizzly entering. He set his pen down and smiled. "All settled in?"

"Yep. I've got a bunk next to Jag's," the bear-man replied, treating himself to a chair.

"What do you think of the new team?"

"Most of them are green behind the ears," Grizzly honestly answered. "I'm surprised they've lasted as long as they have." He paused. "Lobo is an egotistical twerp. Raphaela should be a nun. Sparrow knows Nature like nobody's business and he's counted coup in Montana, but he's not exactly a professional fighter. Madsen, on the other hand, is one of the best. I saw the guy practicing his draw and his speed is incredible. Except for him, you've got a bunch of beginners."

"Don't underestimate them. They pull their own weight."

"I didn't come here to talk about the scout troop," Grizzly noted.

"What can I do for you?"

The bear-man gave the giant a probing look. "Steve Havoc told me that General Gallagher was here earlier."

"He was. So?"

"So?" Grizzly snapped, almost rising in his agitation. "Why the hell didn't you tell me?"

"I didn't think his visit was important," Blade said, the statement sounding lame even to him.

Now Grizzly did rise and move to the front of the desk, his features contorted in unbridled hatred. "Not important? That son of a bitch broke up Athena and me! If he hadn't meddled in our lives she would still be alive. I owe him and you know it."

Blade nodded slowly. "And what about your promise?"

"I knew you'd bring that up."

"You gave me your word," Blade stressed.

Scowling, Grizzly angrily began pacing back and forth, his hands clenching and unclenching again and again, his gaze on the giant. "And naturally you're going to hold me to it?"

"Of course," Blade said, mentally drifting back over a week ago, to the day after they'd left Mesaville, as they'd trekked across the burning desert with miles and miles of sand and rock stretching before them. He'd glanced at the hybrid and said, "I'd like to ask a favor of you."

"Anything," Grizzly had responded. "You know that."

"I want you to promise that you won't kill Gallagher on sight once we get back to California."

The bear-man had stopped in surprise. "You don't know what you're asking."

"And I want your pledge that you won't go hunting him down either."

"You're crazy."

Halting, Blade had placed his hand on the hybrid's shoulder. "For me, Grizzly. Please."

"You'd better have a damn good reason."

"I have several," Blade had told him. "First and foremost is that we don't have any concrete proof of Gallagher's activities. With Havoc and Athena gone we can't make a formal case against him."

"I don't care," Grizzly had snarled. "I want the sucker dead."

"If you go out and kill him the minute we get back, the California authorities will charge you with murder. They'll want to arrest you and throw you in prison."

"Let them try."

"What will you do? Head into the Outlands again and stay there the rest of your life? How long would you last?"

The bear-man had shrugged. "Long enough."

"Don't kid yourself. You're not an animal and you don't deserve to live like one," Blade had said, and paused. "Grizzly, I want Gallagher as much as you do. But I want to learn the reason he's done all this to us—"

"He's a conniving, egotistical bastard. What other reason does he need?"

"And he's also one of the highest-ranking men in the California military, with an excellent service record. He's accustomed to obeying orders even when he doesn't like them. His loyalty has earned him the status of a confidant of the governor's."

"Big deal."

"There must be a better explanation for Gallagher's behavior. I want to learn what it is."

Grizzly had sighed. "You know, if anyone else asked me to do what you are, I'd tell them to go take a flying leap."

"I know."

For over a minute Grizzly had simply bowed his head, deep in thought. At last he'd looked into the Warrior's eyes. "All right. For you I'll do it. I won't kill that scumbag the minute I see him."

"And you won't go hunting for him either?"

"Not until you give me the word."

"Fair enough," Blade had said, smiling.

"Just one thing."

"What?"

"Don't take too long. I don't know how long I can control myself."

The reminiscence came to an end and Blade stared at his friend, noting the torment in the hybrid's face, his heart going out to him.

"I want you to let me off the hook," Grizzly now demanded.

"I can't do that."

"You must!" Grizzly said, twisting and pounding the desktop in fury. "I thought I could stop myself from going after him, but I can't. Just knowing he was here today makes me see red."

"I won't let you out of your promise," Blade said. "If you want to break it, that's your decision. But I don't think you're the type to go back on your word."

"Damn you," Grizzly declared, stiffening. He stormed to the door and stopped to gaze over his shoulder. "I'll give you one week to learn what you want to know. One week. After that time all bets are off."

The door almost snapped off its hinges when he slammed it.

CHAPTER SIX

At ten A.M. the next morning the phone rang. Engrossed in the tedious task of preparing the monthly personnel report for Governor Melnick, who would report on the progress of the recruits to the Federation leaders at the next Council, Blade idly lifted the receiver and mumbled, "Hello."

"Blade? This is Gallagher."

The Warrior became completely alert. "General. What can I do for you?"

"I phoned to let you know the training session has been set up as you wanted."

"Training session?" Blade repeated, striving to recall when he'd made such a request.

"Yes," Gallagher stated stiffly. "Don't you remember? About a month before you took off for Mesaville you asked me if I could arrange a mock combat training session with a Ranger unit. You said something about your people needing experience against seasoned troops."

The reminder jarred Blade's memory. "Oh, that," he said, wondering why it had taken nearly six weeks for the session to be arranged.

As if he was a mind reader, Gallagher provided a plausible answer. "It took so long because the seasoned Ranger units have all been busy on the eastern border fighting the Hell's Bandits."

"Who?"

"A large band of bikers has been raiding our northeast border towns for the past couple of months. They have a hideout somewhere in northwestern Nevada. Whenever they feel like it they just swoop into one of our settlements, kill and loot to their heart's content, then head back into Nevada before our units can catch them."

"Why didn't you tell me about this sooner?"

"Why should I? The last time we had a problem with raiders, the Devils of the Baja, you weren't very pleased when I asked you to help eliminate them."

Blade let the implied slur pass. He'd had a perfectly valid reason for not wanting to involve the Force in the search for the Devils, as the general well knew. The team had just been reformed when Gallagher presented the proposal, and Blade had felt they simply weren't ready to function as a unit.

"Anyway," Gallagher went on, "one of the top Ranger platoons is enjoying a little R & R before going back out in the field. They're currently being housed at March Air Force Base. I spoke with their captain a while ago, and he was delighted at the idea of pitting his boys against your morons."

"Keep it up," Blade said.

"How does tomorrow morning at eight strike you?"

"Where will this session take place?"

"Have you ever heard of Dutchman Canyon?"

"Can't say that I have."

"It's about forty miles west of the Force Facility, deep in the Los Padres National Forest. Got its name ages ago, back in the days of the prospectors. The military has been using the canyon and the adjacent area as a training ground since shortly after the war. It's rugged and remote, perfect for your purposes," General Gallagher detailed.

"Sounds ideal," Blade admitted.

"If you agree, I'll have a company truck there to pick up your team at six A.M. It's a long drive to Dutchman Canyon along winding back roads most of the way. Figure on the trip taking ninety minutes."

"The Force will be ready," Blade said.

"Good. Captain Denison and his people will meet you there. There will also be four officers who will serve as judges during the exercise. They'll rate the performance of both units, attach kill tags, and make certain the practice goes by the book."

"Fine."

"Then I'll call Denison and let him know it's all set up," the general stated.

"One more thing," Blade added.

"What?"

The Warrior smirked and declared, "Grizzly sends his love."

"Screw you."

Blade chuckled as the dial tone replaced the officer, and hung up. His mood turned somber as he contemplated the projected exercise. On the surface it sounded ideal, but he couldn't help but speculate that there might be an ulterior motive lurking behind the general's sudden concern over the squad's need for more training.

Deciding he needed fresh air, Blade rose and walked outside. Except for a few puffy white clouds the sky was clear and bright. He squinted at the sun, then turned as someone hailed him.

"Blade! Blade!"

The Warrior saw Sergeant Havoc running toward him from the northwest. "What's the matter?"

"Doc Madsen sent me to get you," the noncom reported. "We found something."

"What?"

"It's on the rear wall of the supply bunker. Come see, sir."

Without further comment Blade sprinted toward the structure. He spied Lobo and Raphaela standing near the northeast corner, looking at the back of the building. Angling to join them, he spotted the others a few yards beyond the corner, doing the same.

"We just found it," Havoc explained. "Security at this site sure is terrible."

Found what? Blade wondered. He discovered the answer when he joined his perplexed companions behind the bunker.

"Who could have done this?" Sparrow Hawk asked.

"Maybe that brat," Lobo said.

Painted in big red letters on the wall were two lines of sloppily scrawled poetry. The paint was quite dry, indicating whoever had written the verse undoubtedly had so during the night. Lacking any punctuation, the message read:

From Khans land where one and one equals three came the anointed of the mighty to slay fiddle-de-dee

"What in the world does that mean?" Lobo inquired of no one special.

"It makes no sense," Raphaela said.

"Then Lobo should understand it," Jag commented, and both he and Grizzly chuckled.

"Up yours, turkeys."

Blade walked to the wall to study the writing closely. Judging by the bizarre style, the note had been composed by a lunatic. None of the letters were the same size, not even those that were the same letter. Instead of being precisely aligned, the words flowed in a wavy pattern, forming a series of humps from end to end.

"First that child yesterday, now this," Doc Madsen said. "I reckon someone is playing games with us."

Raphaela moved over to the Warrior. "Have you any idea what this is all about?"

"Not a clue," Blade confessed.

Sergeant Havoc cleared his throat. "I'm new on this team and all, but it seems to me that we should take measures to guarantee this doesn't happen again."

"Like what?" Doc asked.

"Oh, like doubling or tripling the sentries. Or maybe we could replace the fence with a higher one."

"Or maybe we should dig holes in the ground and hide in them at night," Jag said.

Havoc mustered a polite smile. "Doesn't it bother you that someone can waltz into the Facility at will and paint cryptic messages without being caught?"

Jag shrugged. "Doesn't affect me one way or the other."

"But this is supposed to be a secure installation," the noncom noted.

"Obviously not secure enough."

"I'm with the new kid," Lobo declared. "I don't like the idea of someone sneakin' up on me in my sleep and slittin' my throat."

"You have nothing to worry about," Jag said.

"I don't?"

"No. Your snoring is bound to scare them off. They'll think we have a lion in the barracks."

"Dipstick."

Blade ran his right hand over several of the letters, feeling the thick consistency of the dried paint. It had an odd satiny sheen, a gloss unlike any he'd ever seen, and contained thin streaks, evidence of the brush strokes used.

"Weird-looking paint," Grizzly remarked, stepping forward and sniffing several times. He recoiled, then sniffed again. "Hey, Jag, get a whiff of this stuff. Tell me that my nose isn't playing tricks on me."

The cat-man complied and exchanged a troubled, knowing glance with his fellow hybrid. "Your nose is working fine. This definitely isn't paint."

Blade touched the substance. "What is it then?"

"Human blood," Grizzly said.

Raphaela gasped.

Removing his hand, Blade stepped back and surveyed the entire wall. From previous experience he knew not to question the hybrid's uncanny sense of smell. If they claimed the substance was blood, then blood it must be. But the quantity involved staggered him. "This would have required a gallon."

"It has to be something else," Raphaela asserted.

Grizzly jabbed a finger at her. "If we say it's blood, lady, it's blood."

Touching his nose to a letter, Jag inhaled several times. "Blood and another liquid. A chemical of some kind would be my guess."

"That tangy odor?" Grizzly said.

"Yeah."

"Why didn't the night patrol spot whoever did this?" Sparrow Hawk asked, "The culprits must have taken fifteen minutes to complete the job."

"Good question," Blade said. "Sparrow, go find Captain Brice, the officer in charge of the Regular Army troops assigned here, and have him report to me on the double. Have him round up and bring every trooper on duty last night."

"On my way," the Flathead said, jogging around the corner.

"Raphaela, you're responsible for cleaning this wall. Lobo and Sergeant Havoc will assist you," Blade instructed.

"Why me?" the Clansman promptly protested.

"Because I said so."

"I didn't sign on with this outfit to be a janitor," Lobo groused.

"If you don't like it here I can always ship you back to the Clan with a note explaining that you think you're too good for the job."

"Boy, do you fight dirty," Lobo said. "I'd have everybody on my case. No, thanks. I'll stay and clean the stinkin' wall."

"Figured you would," Blade responded, and looked at the hybrids. "Make a sweep of the Facility. Look for tracks, check for unusual scents, search for anything out of the ordinary that might give us some idea of who or what did this."

"Who or *what*?" Grizzly repeated. "Do you know something we don't?"

"No. But it's obvious that girl we saw yesterday wasn't human. Whatever we're dealing with is unlike anything we've encountered before."

"We'll go over every square foot," Jag promised, and the pair of animal-men hastened to the north.

Blade turned and headed for the command bunker.

"Hold on there, pardner."

The Warrior halted and shifted as the team's resident gunfighter ambled up to him. "What can I do for you, Doc?"

"You've got it all backwards," Madsen said, his thumbs casually hooked in his gun belt. "You gave everyone orders except me. What can I do? I hate to stand around twiddling my thumbs."

"Thanks for reminding me," Blade said. "You can

come to my office in ten minutes to sign the paperwork."

"What paperwork?"

"The forms necessary to install you formally as my second-in-command."

For the first time since the Warrior and the Cavalryman met, Doc Madsen displayed genuine surprise. "Now hold on a second. When did you get this brainstorm?"

"I need someone to fill Mike Havoc's shoes and you're the logical choice."

Madsen shook his head. "You're loco. I'm not the commanding type. Why not pick Steve? He's got a military background."

Blade glanced at the noncom, who, along with Raphaela and Lobo, was walking toward the entrance to the supply bunker. "He's not experienced enough for the job."

"And what makes you think I am?"

"I know you," Blade said, and started to leave.

"Not so fast," Doc said, clearly perturbed. "If you know me, then you know I'm essentially a loner. I've never given orders in my life."

"You were in charge while I was in the Outlands and you did a fine job," Blade mentioned.

"Big deal. All we were doing was sitting on our fannies waiting for you to get back."

"Even so, I believe you're the best man for the job. Maybe you don't have a service background like Steve Havoc, but you've been in more life-or-death fights than he has, than all the rest of the team combined. You don't lose your head in combat. I've seen you in action, remember? You're decisive and dependable. So unless you beg me not to, I'm appointing you as my second-in-command."

The gunfighter pondered for a bit, then grinned self-consciously. "I'm not the begging type."

"Then I'll see you in ten minutes," Blade said, smiling,

and continued to his office. He had every confidence in Madsen's ability. While the gunman didn't have Special Forces or Regular Army training, Madsen did possess the most important attribute of any leader: the ability to command respect. No one, not even Lobo, would give the Cavalryman a hard time.

Blade came to his door and pushed it open. He stepped into the darkened interior and halted, puzzled, certain he'd left the lights on when he went out. The switch was to his right. He turned, reached for it, and suddenly discovered he wasn't alone.

From the rear came a raspy snarl. A pair of strong hands gripped the Warrior's shoulders, sharp claws dug through his vest into his flesh, and the next instant he was flung bodily into the depths of the room.

CHAPTER SEVEN

It all happened so rapidly that Blade had scant time to react. His legs struck a chair, upending him, tumbling him a good ten feet until he struck the far wall with jarring impact. The prodigious strength of his unknown assailant, combined with the snarl and the claws, convinced him that his adversary must be a hybrid of some sort.

He shoved upright and whipped both Bowies out. The light coming in the doorway provided him illumination in the center of the room, but the walls were plunged in inky shadows. A strange scent assailed his nostrils, a sickeningly sweet stench resembling that of pure honey, one amplified a thousand times.

A whisper of movement occured on the left.

Blade swiveled, the big knives extended, ready for another assault.

Someone laughed, a tittering utterance from the heart of wickedness. "You're going to die, Warrior."

The low voice brought an immediate shock of recognition. It sounds like Jag! Blade thought. But it couldn't be!

A darting form materialized out of the gloom, hurtling straight at the giant.

Blade had a fleeting impression of feline features, and then the creature slammed into him, bowling him over. He found himself flat on his back with his attacker on top. The thing's hands clamped onto his wrists, preventing him from employing the Bowies.

"What now, weakling?" the hybrid mocked him.

The Warrior tried to surge erect. Incredibly, the creature held him down. He could barely distinguish its features, but what little he saw bore an uncanny resemblance to Jaguarundi.

"Cat got your tongue?" the creature asked, and cackled.

Blade didn't waste precious time answering. He didn't know what was going on, didn't know why the thing simply didn't kill him and be done with it. But he wasn't going to look the proverbial gift horse in the mouth. He swept his right knee up and in, connecting with his foe's spine.

The beast arched its back and abruptly let go. Hissing savagely, it leaped to the left into the ring of darkness.

In a smooth motion the Warrior rose, crouching and scanning the office. Since the creature knew where he was, he saw no reason to keep silent. "Don't leave yet. I'm just getting warmed up."

"Enjoy your humor while you can," came a response from near the door. "I'll be back to finish the job."

"Who are you?" Blade demanded.

"One for all and all for one," the thing replied, and raced from the hall.

For a moment Blade saw it silhouetted in the doorway and there could be no mistake. It *was* Jag, or else the hybrid's twin. He ran to the steps, but the creature had already fled out the upper door. Hoping to catch a glimpse of it, he ran to the top, almost colliding with someone about to enter the bunker just as he emerged.

"Whoa! What's the rush?" Doc Madsen inquired, stepping back to avoid being knocked down. "First him, now you."

"Who?" Blade asked, looking in all directions.

"Jag," Doc said, nodding at the southwest corner. "He headed thataway as if his loincloth was on fire."

The Warrior raced to the side of the command bunker, disappointed to find the swift hybrid was gone, probably into the trees to the north. "Damn," he said, venting his frustration.

"What the heck is going on?" Doc asked, joining him. "Are you positive you saw Jag?"

"What do you take me for? Of course," Doc said. "I was coming over to talk to you about my being second-in-command when he came tearing out of the bunker. He grinned at me, then ran off."

"Did he say anything?"

"Nope. I said howdy but he didn't answer." Doc stared at the giant's shoulder. "Hey, what happened to you?"

Blade looked down at the holes in his vest and the blood trickling from both shoulders. "Jag, or whoever that was, attacked me." He couldn't believe it had really been his friend, but the testimony of his own eyes and Doc's eyewitness confirmation refuted his wishful thinking, seeming to confirm the unthinkable.

"I'll phone the guards and have them scour the grounds for an intruder," the gunfighter said, and sped into the bunker.

Despite the pain he felt, Blade chuckled. For someone who didn't want to be promoted, Doc Madsen exhibited the ideal efficiency a second-in-command should possess. He leaned against the building, contemplating the seemingly senseless attack and what to do about it.

There had to be a connection between the incident involving the little girl, the verse on the supply bunker, and this latest inexplicable assault, but for the life of him he couldn't identify the linking thread. It was was if someone planned to keep the Force in turmoil, intending to confuse them with a continuous stream of bizarre events. But *why?*

He recalled his prior belief that someone was playing games with them, a belief Doc had echoed. If so, the Force was being set up for something, but what? Absently glancing at the woods, he saw one of the hybrids appear.

Grizzly gave a friendly wave and approached. When still a dozen yards off his keen eyes detected the torn vest and the blood. He promptly sprinted to the corner. "What happened to you?"

"Where's Jag?" Blade rejoined.

"What? I don't know. We separated," Grizzly answered. "Why?"

The Warrior explained.

"Impossible," the bear-man stated when he finished. "Jag would never jump you."

Blade gingerly placed his right hand on his sore left shoulder. "These holes aren't figments of my imagination."

"I'd better go find him," Grizzly said, beginning to turn.

"No."

Grizzly looked at the giant in surprise. "But he could be in trouble."

"No," Blade repeated firmly. "The troopers will do it."

At that moment Doc Madsen returned on the double, a first-aid kit in his left hand. "I spoke to Sergeant Gifford and ordered him to search the compound."

"Who died and made you a general?" Grizzly joked.

"I did," Blade said. "Doc is my new adjutant." He

looked at the gunman. "Call the guard station again and find out what's keeping Sparrow and Captain Brice. They should have been here by now."

"Okay," Doc said, handing over the kit before hastening back into the command bunker.

"Why him?" Grizzly inquired.

"Did you want the job?"

"No. I wouldn't make a good leader. I'd always be letting my claws do my thinking for me," Grizzly said, and glanced at the forest. "I really think I should go after Jag."

"I know how you feel about him but the answer is still no."

"Why not?"

"I have my reasons."

"Are you worried that whoever attacked you will come after me?"

"Something like that."

"I'd rip the sucker to shreds."

"Probably. But you're still not going into the woods and that's final."

The bear-man frowned and shook his head in disapproval. "Sometimes you can be a cold SOB."

Ten minutes later Jaguarundi finally showed up.

Blade stood behind the supply bunker, clutching his vest in his left hand, and watched Lobo, Doc, Sparrow, Havoc, and Grizzly wipe off the last of the blood. He twisted repeatedly to stare at the trees.

"Will you hold still, darn it?" Raphaela complained, trying to dab medicine on the holes. "You're too big. It's hard enough for me to see what I'm doing without you moving all the time."

"Sorry."

"You should have let me do this sooner," Raphaela

VENGEANCE STRIKE 71

chided him while wiping dried blood from his left shoulder.

"Couldn't be helped," Blade said, thinking of the discussion he'd had with Captain Brice and the night guards five minutes ago. No one had seen anything out of the ordinary. Every few hours between dusk and dawn patrols had gone past the bunkers, yet whoever had written the verse had cleverly eluded detection.

"You're like all men," Raphaela said.

"Meaning?"

"Men always have to prove how tough they are, and they always do it at the dumbest times. I knew a guy once who had the flu, yet still wanted to take his girlfriend on a moonlit stroll."

"He was being romantic."

"He was an idiot. The temperature outside had dropped to forty below and three feet of snow covered the ground."

"Look who's coming," Lobo declared, pointing at the woods.

The Warrior spotted the cat-man hurrying toward them. "That's enough for now," he told Raphaela, and quickly donned the vest. The rest gathered around, compelling him to remark, "I'll handle this."

"Jag is innocent," Raphaela stated. "Suspecting him is foolish."

"I saw him run from the bunker," Doc reminded her.

They fell silent, watching the hybrid. Jaguarundi slowed, his forehead creasing, looking at each of them in turn. "What's up?" he asked when only ten feet away.

"Where have you been?" Blade demanded.

The hard tone brought Jag up short. "In the forest searching for sign," he replied. "Why? And why are all of you staring at me like I'm some kind of monster?"

"You've been there this whole time?" Blade asked skeptically. "Grizzly came back fifteen minutes ago."

Jag reached up to touch the back of his head. "Has it been that long? Somebody knocked me out after Grizzly and I separated to check different parts of the forest. I just revived."

Lobo snorted. "Likely story, Fur Face. Do you have any proof of this fairy tale?"

"Lobo," Blade warned, "*I'll* take care of this."

"Geez, I'm just trying to help."

"Zip it," Blade snapped. He walked over to Jag. "Someone jumped me in my office while you were gone."

The cat-man stiffened. "Who was it?"

"You."

Evidently thinking the reply was a joke of some sort, Jag began to grin. Then the Warrior's grave expression sank home. "Me? Are you crazy?"

Blade lifted the top of his vest. "See for yourself."

Leaning forward, Jag examined the wounds, then raised his right hand to thoughtfully regard the pointed inch-long fingernails that served as his claws. "Those holes are exactly the kind I would have made."

"Or did make," Lobo declared.

Jag gazed into the Warrior's eyes. "I didn't attack you. You must believe me."

"I'd like to," Blade admitted, "but we have a slight problem. A witness saw you running from the command bunker."

"What?" Jag declared in disbelief.

Doc Madsen stepped closer. "Sorry, friend. But I saw you clear as day."

"This can't be happening," Jag said softly, pressing a palm to his forehead. "You know I would never hurt any of you."

"Tell us about the knock on your head," Blade directed.

"There's not much to tell. Grizzly and I decided we could search the woods faster if we split up. I went to

VENGEANCE STRIKE 73

the west, and as I jogged past a tree someone leaped out and hit me. Felt as if they used a crowbar. That's all I remember until I heard voices and woke up to find a patrol about twenty yards away. Naturally I came straight here."

Lobo laughed. "Do you expect us to buy this bull?"

The Warrior had reached the limit of his patience. He spun on his heel and glared at the Clansman. "Five laps around the bunkers right now. Get going."

"You're kiddin'?" Lobo responded.

"Do I *look* like I'm kidding?"

"No, you look like you want to stomp my butt."

"Then take your pick."

"Five laps it is," Lobo said, peeved, and reluctantly began jogging. "But if you ask me, this is a pitiful way for the heartthrob of the Clan to be spendin' his time."

Blade faced the cat-man. "Now where were we? Oh, yeah. You claim you were struck and knocked out. Let me check your head."

Jaguarundi bent at the waist.

Slowing running his right hand over the hybrid's skull, his palm tickled by the short reddish hair, Blade tried to find evidence of a lump or a cut. There was none. "Okay, thanks," he said, lowering his arm.

"You don't believe me, do you?" Jag asked, straightening.

"I want to," Blade stated. "But as head of the Force I can't allow my personal feelings to influence my judgment. I must do what is best for the unit as a whole. With a cloud of suspicion hanging over your head, I'm afraid I must place you under arrest."

"Arrest?" Jag repeated nervously, glancing at his teammates.

"House arrest," Blade elaborated. "You'll be confined to the barracks until further notice. Tomorrow morning we're participating in a training exercise with a Ranger platoon. You'll stay here. By the time we get back I should have my mind made up about whether to file formal charges or kick you off the squad."

A low growl rumbled from Grizzly's throat and he stormed up to the Warrior. "Kick Jag off the squad? Without any proof that he's the one who jumped you? If you do, you can kiss me good-bye also."

"We'll discuss this tomorrow," Blade said stiffly, and headed for the command bunker. "Jag, I'd like to see you in my office."

"Sure," the cat-man said, gazing quizzically at the Warrior's wide shoulders. "I'll be there in a minute."

Grizzly laid a hand on his friend's arm. "Don't worry. Everything will work out. I'll get to the bottom of this if it's the last thing I ever do."

"Thank you."

The bear-man looked at the giant heading for the bunker. "I knew he'd changed a lot in the past year, but I didn't realize how much until this moment. He's let the job go to his head. Someone should take him down a peg or three."

"Don't be too hard on him."

"How can you defend a guy who just stabbed you in the back?" Grizzly asked angrily. "After all the time you've worked together, he should trust you completely. Instead, he has you under house arrest. It's an insult!"

Jag scratched his chin, still staring at the Warrior. "Blade never does anything without a good reason. Don't take it personally."

"You've got it all backwards. You're the one who should be offended."

"I'm not, though. So please don't hold this against Blade," Jag said, and walked after the giant.

Raphaela and Havoc joined the bear-man.

"I think Blade is being unfair," the Molewoman commented.

"You and me both," Grizzly agreed.

"I don't know," Sergeant Havoc said. "He's doing the only thing he can under the circumstances. None of us can trust Jag until he proves his innocence."

"Who asked you?" Grizzly snapped. He stalked off to the south, glowering at the world in general.

"I didn't mean to upset him," Havoc said.

"Then you shouldn't be so thoughtless," Raphaela chided, and ran to catch Grizzly.

Sergeant Havoc critically regarded both of them. He sighed, made a clucking sound, and shook his head before heading toward the barracks. "Thoughtless?" he said under his breath, and snickered.

CHAPTER EIGHT

A subdued and sullen Force, with one notable exception, waited outside the barracks the next morning at ten minutes until six for the convoy truck to arrive. No one spoke. Everyone except Sergeant Havoc wore a glum expression. They were all bothered by Jaguarundi's predicament, and had stayed awake late the night before discussing the situation. After the varied hardships the group had confronted and triumphed over, they'd grown to respect and like one another, making the very idea that one of their own stood accused of betraying the team a personal affront to each member.

Raphaela and the noncoms wore camouflage fatigues. The rest wore their normal attire. Everyone other than Grizzly carried an M-16 slung over a shoulder.

When Blade emerged from the command bunker at five minutes until six only Sergeant Havoc tendered a greeting. The Warrior also had an M-16. He went into the barracks, spoke briefly with Jaguarundi, and returned just as the truck arrived.

A lone private drove the vehicle. He waited until they were all loaded in the bed before executing a U-turn and

VENGEANCE STRIKE 77

driving to the gate. Once out of the Facility he accelerated rapidly, the vehicle's big tires whipping clouds of dust in its wake.

The truck took a series of back roads until it reached I-5. Turning south, it proceeded to the turnoff at Saugas, and bore westward until reaching Highway 150. At the junction it turned to the north, following the winding road to Highway 33. A right turn soon brought them to the Los Padres National Forest, where the road curved and twisted continually, forcing the driver to shift constantly and go slow. Ten miles past Beaver Creek the driver made a right onto a narrow dirt road, little better than a track, that wound far into the forest.

Not one of the Force bothered to speak during all this time. Many were the irate glances cast at the Warrior, but he appeared not to notice.

It took them 20 minutes to travel five miles. A bright red sign at the side of the road informed all and sundry that they were approaching a Free State of California Military Area, and in five more miles passage would be restricted to military personnel.

The last five miles went the slowest, with the road hemmed in by high trees and thick undergrowth. Numerous potholes filled the roadway and the truck somehow managed to hit every one. When the downshifting of the gears and the application of the brakes eventually heralded their arrival at the exercise site, one of the team broke the silence.

"About friggin' time," Lobo said. "My kidneys are killin' me. Another mile and I'd pee my pants."

"You can be crude at times," Raphaela said.

"Hey, when a man's got to go, a man's got to go," the Clansman retorted.

Blade, seated at the rear of the bed next to the gate, surveyed his people and said, "I want all of you to be on your best behavior. That goes double for you, Lobo."

"Since when have I ever caused trouble, dude?"

"I've already explained about the nature of this exercise," Blade went on. "We'll be pitted against a crack Ranger unit. I don't know the details yet, but I have confidence in each and every one of you. Do your best and we'll come out on top."

"Even without Jag?" Grizzly asked resentfully.

The Warrior didn't bother to acknowledge the crack. He braced his legs as the convoy truck lurched to a stop, then let down the gate and jumped to the grass. "Everyone out," he commanded. "You know the drill."

In single file the team imitated the giant's example and formed into a row, standing at attention.

Blade walked around the side of the truck and saw the driver glancing out the window at him.

"General Gallagher gave me orders to drop you guys off and head back," the man said. "Another truck must be coming to pick you up this afternoon."

"Most likely," Blade said, surveying their vicinity.

A wide clearing had been carved out of the woods. The road ended abruptly at a pair of trees bearing large signs warning that trespassers were not permitted past that point. A small, locked shack stood to the right of the trees. Otherwise, there were no facilities of any kind, nothing to indicate the area was used regularly.

"See you around," the driver said, and turned the truck about. He waved as he drove off.

The Warrior turned to his team. "At ease," he declared.

"Where the hell are we?" Lobo inquired, gazing apprehensively at the shadowy woods. "You didn't say anything about this exercise takin' place in the middle of nowhere."

"Don't you like the outdoors?" Raphaela teased.

"I'm a city boy, sweetheart, not a cave man," Lobo

said, and glanced at the giant. "Hey, can I take that leak now or what?"

"Go right ahead," Blade said. He rotated in a circle, noting the verdant vegetation, the oaks and maples and sycamores that formed an uneven canopy over the underbrush, the periodic pines of several varieties, the many shrubs and smaller plants. Birds chirped constantly and flitted from here to there while a few squirrels scampered along high limbs. The remote ruggedness of the area was borne out by the lack of fear the wildlife displayed for the human invaders.

"We have company," Doc suddenly announced.

An officer walked toward them from out of the trees. He wore the insignia of a lieutenant and carried a clipboard in his left hand. Above his left shirt pocket was a small card bearing a single word in large black letters: JUDGE.

Blade went to meet him. "Hello. You must be one of the four officers who will evaluate the exercise."

"Yes," the man said. "Lieutenant Wharton at your service." He shook hands and nodded to the east. "Captain Denison and his men are already here and in position. The other judges have been stationed at appropriate points throughout the exercise area. Whenever you're ready, we can begin."

"How is the exercise to be conducted?"

"No one has told you yet?"

"No."

"Typical," Lieutenant Wharton muttered. "Where the military is concerned, sometimes the right hand doesn't know what the left hand is doing."

Blade grinned.

"Anyway, here's the way this will work," Wharton said. "The twelve Rangers have been divided into four squads and sent out into Dutchman Canyon. You're supposed to divide your people up and go find them. It's as simple as that."

"General Gallagher mentioned something about kill tags. Shouldn't we be issued blanks for the mock combat?"

"Didn't your driver give you the blanks?" Wharton asked.

"Nope."

"Damn it all. He was to provide them," the officer declared testily. "Someone will pay for this inefficiency."

"Maybe we can make do without them."

"I suppose. All you have to do is say 'bang-bang' and the judge will rule the shoot valid."

"The Rangers do have their blanks?" Blade queried.

"Yes," Wharton assured him, and consulted his watch. "It's eight-fifteen. As soon as you're ready we can get this show on the road."

"Okay. Let me divide up the Force," Blade said, and he walked over to them. "I take it that all of you heard?"

"Every detail," Sparrow Hawk responded. "Quite frankly, I'm amazed the white man ever drove my ancestors from their homeland."

"Listen up," Blade said. "We'll work in pairs. Doc, you and Sparrow will be together. Grizzly, it will be you and Raphaela. Sergeant Havoc will go with me."

"What about Lobo?" Raphaela wondered.

Blade scanned the trees. "Where is he, by the way?"

"Trying to figure out how his pecker works," Grizzly remarked.

The object of the bear-man's sarcasm came out of the woods wiping his hand at a wet spot on his pants.

"What a moron," Grizzly quipped. "I don't want him on my team."

"I'll take him if you insist," Doc said.

"I insist," Blade stated, and waited for the Clansman to join them. "Lobo, you're on Doc's team."

VENGEANCE STRIKE

"Team? What's going on?"

"Doc and Sparrow will explain," Blade said, and glanced over his shoulder to ensure the lieutenant couldn't overhear before lowering his voice conspiratorially. "Pay attention. I'll only say this once." He paused, pleased they were glued to his every word. "I suspect there's more to this exercise than we've been told, but I have no idea what we're in store for. Stay alert. Watch your backs. Don't let the Rangers get the drop on you. And trust no one. Understood?"

"I don't understand any of this," Lobo said. "You make it sound like this is for real."

"For all we know it might well be."

The severity with which the Warrior uttered the statement caused the Force members to exchange perplexed expressions. Blade double-checked the lieutenant and continued speaking in an urgent, low voice.

"It's about time all of you knew the truth, or at least as much of it as I know. General Gallagher has been trying in subtle ways to have our team disbanded. So far he's failed, but he's bound to try another stunt soon, possibly today during the exercise. So trust no one. I can't emphasize it enough."

Lieutenant Wharton interrupted the revelation by calling out, "Are you all set? We should start as soon as we can."

Blade let his gaze linger on each one of his people, confirming by their somber countenances that they fully appreciated the gravity of his disclosure. He turned and nodded at the officer. "We're all set."

Wharton came over. "Okay. I'll fill you in on the rules." He shifted and pointed to the east, at the large signs. "A trail begins near those signs. Follow it for about a quarter of a mile and you'll come to Dutchman Canyon. The exercise will take place within the canyon boundaries."

"How big is this canyon?" Grizzly asked.

"It's fourteen miles long and averages three miles wide," Wharton informed them, and grinned. "Don't worry. There's plenty of room to conduct war games. And you won't have to worry over straying out of bounds because the canyon walls serve as the boundaries. The Rangers will be the defenders in this exercise while your team will take the offensive. If the Rangers spot you first, they'll open fire using blanks and a judge will attach red kill tags to anyone who is slain. If you spot them first, you'll have to pretend you fire your weapons since none of you were issued blanks." He paused. "Any questions?"

"Yeah," Grizzly said. "Who thinks up these stupid games?"

The officer ignored the hybrid. He noted the time, made a notation on his clipboard, and looked at the Warrior. "You can hike to the canyon now. I need to go on ahead to reach my observation post in time."

"One thing," Blade said. "We weren't told to bring any rations. I take it that we're not to take any food or water during the exercise?"

Wharton blinked. "No. But it should be over by this afternoon and a truck will be here by then to take everyone back." He smiled. "Good luck." Wheeling, he hurried to the east and vanished in the woods.

"What a nice man," Raphaela said.

"He's a dork," Lobo disagreed. "All Army clowns are dorks."

"That's enough out of you," Blade stated, glancing at Sergeant Havoc. The noncom was watching a robin in a nearby tree. Blade headed out. "Fall in. And I don't want any talking."

For once they listened, remaining perfectly quiet during the hike to the mouth of Dutchman Canyon. More signs warned the public to keep out at all costs and detailed legal punishments and fines for those who were caught violating the law.

Blade rested his hands on his Bowies and surveyed the wondrous work of Nature. He'd seen photographs in books in the Family library of the magnificent Grand Canyon, and while Dutchman Canyon could hardly compare in scope and grandeur, in many respects it resembled its mightier relative.

The rock walls reared hundreds of feet high, forming impassable barriers that essentially shut off the canyon from the outside world on three sides. Sunlight glinted off the rock, accenting the many weather-carved lines and glistening layers of quartz. Along the canyon floor grew prolific vegetation watered by a stream that flowed out of a spring at the base of the north wall near the mouth and meandered eastward down the center of the canyon. It was a veritable Garden of Paradise, and the animal life was abundant. A herd of deer was visible grazing on a low hill on the south side of the stream, and birds of every description were flitting from perch to perch. Many large boulders, stone spires, and erosion-worn columns dotted the landscape.

"This is beautiful," Raphaela said in awe.

"Beauty can be deceptive," Blade reminded her. "Don't let your guard down for a minute."

"Can we waste these Rangers if they try anything?" Grizzly inquired.

"Only if absolutely necessary," Blade said, and gestured at the canyon. "We'll split up here. Grizzly and Raphaela will take the north side. Doc, Sparrow, and Lobo will take the south. Havoc and I will stick with the stream."

"It figures you get the water," Lobo muttered.

"I imagine that all of us will be too busy to think about drinking," Blade said, and unslung his M-16. "Take care of yourselves," he cautioned.

"Don't worry about us, dude," Lobo said. He thumped on his chest. "The Rangers don't stand a chance against a lean, mean, fightin' machine like me."

"You're probably right," Grizzly agreed, and looked at the Warrior. "Do we win if the Rangers laugh themselves to death?"

The giant moved into the canyon. "Head out. And do your best to stay alive."

CHAPTER NINE

Doc Madsen, Sparrow Hawk, and Lobo hiked half a mile to the south before turning eastward, moving cautiously through thick undergrowth, their soles barely making any sound on the spongy carpet of grass and leaves underfoot. Overhead were the spreading branches of the many trees, blocking the sunlight and casting gray shadows over everything. Birds sang all around them, and occasionally rabbits bounded from their path.

The gunfighter halted and adjusted the M-16's sling over his left shoulder. He moved the flap of his frock coat aside to expose his prized Magnum, permitting an unobstructed draw in an emergency. "Sparrow, you should take the point," he said softly.

"Why can't I?" Lobo asked.

"Because Sparrow is at home in the wild. You're not. You said so yourself."

"No offense, my friend," the Flathead said to the Clansman, "but in the forest you have all the finesse of a pregnant buffalo."

Lobo snorted. "Shows how much you know, dummy. Men can't get pregnant."

Sparrow rolled his eyes and walked ahead 20 feet. Like the Cavalryman, he had his M-16 over a shoulder and his preferred weapon of choice, the spear that had been his father's grasped in both hands. He nodded at Doc, and they resumed their search for Rangers.

The minutes dragged by. No unusual sounds were heard and nothing out of the ordinary occurred.

When they came to the same hill on which the deer had been grazing they found the animals gone. Skirting the open space where the tender grass grew, they reached a jumbled cluster of boulders near the summit and halted.

"These Rangers are very competent," Sparrow remarked in a whisper. "There has been no sign of them, not even footprints."

"Strange," Doc remarked.

"I have an idea," Lobo said. "Why don't we stay here for a few hours, then head on back and tell the Big Guy we never saw any of the soldier boys?"

Doc glanced at him. "You're not serious?"

"The hell I'm not. I could use a nap right about now to catch up on my beauty sleep. It's unhealthy for a person to roll out of the sack before the sun does."

"The sun was up when you awoke," Sparrow mentioned.

"Just barely," Lobo said, and grinned at them. "What do you say? Can we take a break?"

"No," Doc replied.

"Terrific. You've only been second-in-command for one day and already you're becoming bossy."

Doc gave the word and they moved out once again, going slowly, taking an hour to travel less than two miles. The next time they paused was beside an enormous oak tree.

"Still no sign of the Rangers?" Doc inquired.

"None," Sparrow answered, his brow knit. "Not so

much as a partial heel print or a scuff mark in the soil. Apparently none of the Rangers came this way."

The gunfighter scanned the woods, reflecting. Sparrow Hawk was one of the best trackers in the Flathead Nation; if he asserted there were no prints, then there were none. But surely some of the Rangers were hiding along the south side of the stream?

Lobo yawned. "This exercise is boring me to tears. I hope the others are havin' better luck."

"We'll move closer to the south wall of the canyon," Doc proposed. "Sooner or later we're bound to cut the Rangers' trail."

Adopting a zigzag partrol pattern, the trio walked for 40 minutes until they arrived at the edge of a meadow. Sparrow stopped first and waited for his friends to join him.

"I saw no evidence of human tracks."

Doc pushed his wide-brimmed hat back on his head and mopped at his forehead. "I don't like this," he declared suspiciously. "Granted, Dutchman Canyon is big, but we should have found something by now."

"Or heard something," Sparrow said, gazing out over the canyon. "Why hasn't there been any shooting yet? Surely Grizzly had located Rangers by this time. His heightened senses would lead him right to them."

"And Blade ain't exactly a slouch either," Lobo mentioned. "Maybe you guys have a point."

"We'll go on in this direction for a little longer," Doc said, "but if we don't locate any Rangers we'll head for the stream and try to find Blade."

Another 15 minutes found them in a field of boulders where many of the huge rocks were the size of trucks. They threaded among the monoliths, a few lizards skittering out of sight at their approach.

"This is a waste of our time," Lobo groused.

Doc was inclined to agree. He speculated on whether the Rangers might have positioned themselves much farther up the canyon, perhaps even at the far end, and decided the soldiers wouldn't have bothered going such a distance, especially since the exercise was supposed to be concluded by the afternoon. A disturbing possibility gnawed at his mind. What if there were no Rangers?

At the end of the boulder field Doc stopped and pointed toward the stream. "Track Blade down, Sparrow."

The Flathead nodded and altered direction.

Soon they were deep in the primeval woods again. A ground squirrel chattered at them for intruding in its territory. A jay vented a raucous cry.

Doc kept an eye on Sparrow, whose point position made him the most vulnerable to ambush. He had trailed the Indian into a stand of saplings, listening to the birds, when suddenly a deathly quiet descended, a total cessation of all noise.

The Flathead and the Cavalryman instantly froze. Lobo, gloomily contemplating the toes of his boots, practically bumped into the gunfighter before he realized they had stopped. His head snapped up, his eyes widening slightly.

Sparrow Hawk, holding the spear level at his waist, the gleaming tip outward, retraced his steps until he stood next to Madsen. "Something is out there," he announced tensely.

Lobo tried to swivel his head 360 degrees. "What kind of something?"

"I don't know."

"Big help you are."

Doc listened, but heard just the breeze rustling the trees. "A mutation, you think?"

"Could be. Definitely a predator," Sparrow said.

"It might be a mountain lion or a bear," Lobo observed. "What's the big deal?"

"Better safe than sorry," Doc said, his right hand on the Smith and Wesson.

"What if it's the Rangers?" Lobo asked.

"It's not," Sparrow responded.

"How do you know?"

"I know."

"Has anyone ever told you that talkin' to you is like talkin' to an echo with a warped sense of humor?"

"Pipe down," Doc directed. He estimated they must be less than half a mile from the stream and decided to make for it. Should there be a predator stalking them, the stream would cut off one avenue of stealthy approach. "Follow me," he said, taking the lead, every nerve vibrant. The saplings, spaced close together, obstructed his view, and eager to get out of them, he quickened his pace.

A large, vague form appeared to the west, just beyond the saplings, gliding a few feet before abruptly disappearing.

"Did you guys see that?" Lobo whispered.

"Yes," Sparrow confirmed.

"Me too," Doc chimed in, not slowing, acutely aware of their disadvantage while hemmed in by the young trees. They needed room to maneuver, to see.

Again the thing materialized, only now to the north, a looming shadow that seemed to be peering in at them. Then it melted away.

"What the hell is that?" Lobo queried anxiously.

Neither of the Clansman's companions replied. They moved to the end of the saplings and found themselves in a small clearing bordered on two sides by a profuse, impenetrable thicket.

"Think it's gone?" Lobo asked.

From the thicket issued a low growl.

Doc's right hand was lightning, the Magnum leaping

clear of his holster, his thumb on the hammer, his finger curled around the trigger. But no target presented itself and the growling promptly ceased.

"I bet if we spray some lead in there the thing will run off," Lobo suggested.

"Save your ammo until we know what it is," Doc said.

A faint crackling of twigs revealed the creature to be on the go, the noise gradually diminishing.

"It's leavin'," Lobo declared happily.

In seconds silence gripped the woods again.

Sparrow Hawk moved closer to the thicket, squatted, and gazed intently into its depths.

"See anything?" Doc asked.

"No. Perhaps the creature truly has gone."

"But maybe it will come back," Doc stated. He jerked his left thumb northward. "Let's skedaddle and not stop until we reach the stream."

"There's no rush," Lobo commented. "Whatever that thing is, it obviously knows better than to mess with us."

Twirling the revolver into his holster, Doc resumed walking. "Or it could have gone to get others of its kind," he said.

"Others?" Lobo repeated, sudden worry on his face. "I never thought of that." He hefted the M-16 and hastened to catch up with the gunfighter. "Wait for me, cowboy. You'll need someone to guard your back if the thing does return."

The Flathead fell in last.

Ten minutes elapsed, ten minutes of hurrying through the almost tropical plant growth, ten minutes of not hearing any wildlife, not even so much as the buzz of an insect. Doc found a game trail bearing the hoofprints of deer and other animal tracks that wound in the direction they were going, and took it, which enabled them to pick up the pace considerably. The trail went under a high stone arch at one point, and as the Cavalryman passed underneath the massive, naturally formed shape his nostrils tingled and he sneezed.

Doc halted, inhaled deeply, and scrunched up his nose. "What's that awful smell?"

The Clansman sniffed and grinned. "I sort of like it."

"You do?" Sparrow said, scenting the air. "It reminds me of honey, only much, much stronger."

"Never smelled anything like it," Doc remarked, continuing their journey.

"We should be near the stream," Sparrow noted.

"Good," Lobo said. "My clodhoppers are killin' me." All three stopped once more when the pounding of feet drew their attention to the left. A huge figure was running directly toward them, barreling through the undergrowth like a thing possessed.

Doc's fingers closed on the Smith and Wesson, and he was about to clear leather when he recognized the figure. He grinned and exclaimed, "It's Blade."

"Where are his Bowies and his M-16?" Sparrow inquired.

The gunfighter tensed, realizing the Hawk-eyed Flathead was right. The Warrior didn't have any weapons. And since Doc knew the giant well enough to know that Blade would never part with those big knives except under the direst of circumstances, he ran to meet the Warrior halfway, his companions at his side.

"Thank goodness all of you are safe," Blade declared as he met them.

"What happened, dude?" Lobo asked.

"Where is Sergeant Havoc?" Sparrow added.

Blade nodded to the west. "We were jumped by a mutation. It sprang out of the brush and knocked me down, stunning me. When I came to the thing was gone." He paused. "It had taken Havoc."

"It also took your weapons?" Sparrow queried.

"Apparently."

"But what use would a mutation have for knives and an assault rifle?" Sparrow asked.

"How should I know?" the Warrior retorted. "Maybe the thing is part human. I didn't get a good look at it, but I do know it was a biped."

"Have you seen Grizzly and Raphaela?" Doc asked.

"No. We'll go find them now," Blade said, and smiled in partial relief. "I was worried that the same creature or another like it might have gotten all of you."

"We saw something earlier," Sparrow disclosed. "But it melted away into the forest before we could identify it."

"There must be several of the things then," Blade stated. "Which could explain why Havoc and I saw no sign of the Rangers."

"You too?" Doc said.

"Yep. We were beginning to think the entire exercise was a sham." Blade pivoted and hiked toward the middle of Dutchman Canyon. "Our best bet is to reach the stream and stick close to it. If we yell our heads off Grizzly and Raphaela should hear and rejoin us."

Doc and the others followed. "Want to borrow my M-16? I don't need it."

"Sure," the Warrior said gratefully and took the rifle. He checked the magazine, nodded, and led them onward.

As the gunfighter trailed the head of the Force he tried to imagine what kind of beast could take the giant by surprise. Although not a mutant, the Warrior possessed remarkable senses that were more acute than most men's and had previously demonstrated an uncanny "sixth sense," an ability to perceive danger where none supposedly existed. Whatever had jumped Blade must have been exceptionally stealthy.

Doc heard a distinct bubbling noise, and within a minute

they were standing on the south bank of the two-foot-deep stream. Small fish swam past them. He sank onto his left knee, dipped his left hand into the chill water, and splashed a handful of the refreshing liquid on his neck and chin.

"Which way?" Sparrow asked.

"West," Blade told them, and marched in that direction.

Dabbing water on his forehead and cheeks, Doc let Lobo and Sparrow pass him. He noticed several swallows winging from the forest on their left toward the trees on the opposite bank. As the birds drew close to the giant they abruptly changed their bearing, flapping their wings wildly and streaking off to the east instead. He chuckled, ascribing their abnormal behavior to an instinctive fear of someone so large.

Rising, the gunfighter brought up the rear. They stayed next to the gradually winding stream until they reached a shallow pool ten feet across. The Warrior halted, placing his hands on his hips. Lobo and Sparrow were right behind him, side by side.

"This should do nicely," Blade said.

"For what, dude?" Lobo asked.

"We'll take a brief break."

Sparrow motioned impatiently with his spear. "But what about Havoc and the rest? Now is not the time to be stopping."

"It is for me," Blade said, facing them and smiling. "I'm tired."

"A muscle-head like you?" Lobo declared.

Blade nodded. "Tired of the subterfuge."

"The what?" Lobo inquired.

"Such a massive physique taxes me tremendously," Blade said, bending down to deposit the M-16 on the ground. Without warning he straightened and lashed out, gripping the Clansman and the Flathead behind their necks. In a brutal exhibition of awesome power he slammed their heads together, their temples cracking loudly, then shoved them aside.

Doc was so shocked that his ordinarily swift reflexes were unequal to the occasion. He saw the giant leaping at him and went for his Magnum, but with only a yard between them he was unable to level the revolver before Blade's brawny right fist smashed into his jaw and a multitude of stars engulfed his consciousness in a swirling celestial vortex that sucked him into an inky limbo.

CHAPTER TEN

Grizzly halted on the crest of a barren knoll to sniff the air. His nostrils flared as he registered the scent of rabbit, squirrel, bobcat, deer, and a lingering trace of mountain lion. He scented dank earth, pine trees, and the many aromas from the varied vegetation, but not so much as a hint of any humans. "Something is wrong here," he announced.

Standing behind him, her M-16 cradled loosely in her arms, Raphaela brushed at her red bangs and asked, "Why?"

"There's no trace of the Rangers."

"Maybe your nose is stuffed up," Raphaela said in all innocence. "This time of year is great for catching colds."

The bear-man gave her a look that implied her sanity was in question. "I don't have a cold," he stated stiffly.

"Is the wind blowing the right way?"

"It keeps shifting," Grizzly said. "I should have picked them up by now."

Raphaela surveyed the long expanse of the beautiful canyon. "Well, they have to be here somewhere. That nice Lieutenant Wharton told us they are."

"Do you believe everything everybody tells you?"

"Of course not," Raphaela said, adopting a defensive tone. "But I don't see why he would have lied to us."

"Remember what Blade told us. We're not to trust anyone."

"Does that include you?" Raphaela asked, and giggled.

Rolling his eyes, the hybrid proceeded to the bottom of the knoll and into a stretch of woods. The Molewoman, he decided, had no business being on the Force. She was as naive as they came, and her inexperience could prove costly in a crisis situation. He wondered why the Warrior permitted her to stay. If the choice had been his he would have sent her packing back to the Moles and told them to send someone more competent.

For that matter, as he'd indicated to Blade, Grizzly wasn't very highly impressed by the new team. Lobo should be given the boot too. Sparrow was all right, but he didn't impress Grizzly as much as the previous volunteer from the Flathead tribe, Thunder-Rolling-in-the-Mountain. Nor was the new guy, Havoc, worth bragging about. He rated the young noncom as a first-rate wienie.

The wind, which had been blowing from the northwest, changed once again, coming from the southeast, then the south, and the southwest. The high canyon walls had a funneling effect on the surface winds, amplifying them and reflecting them back out the mouth of the canyon.

Grizzly's sensitive nose detected a new odor, a faint, puzzling, sickening sweet fragrance. He paused, inhaling deeply, but the wind shifted once more before he could get a fix on where the sweet scent came from.

"Do you smell the Rangers?" Raphaela inquired.

"Something else. It's gone now," Grizzly revealed, moving on.

"Mind if we talk a bit?"

Typical human, Grizzly thought, yet he replied politely.

"Yes. We're on a combat exercise, or have you forgotten?"

"No. But if, as you claim, the Rangers aren't anywhere around, what harm can it do?"

Grizzly made a mental note to pair off with Lobo next time. "Okay. Just keep your voice down." He glanced over his right shoulder and saw her grinning. "What do you want to talk about?"

"You."

"Forget it. The subject is taboo."

"How are we to get to know you if you won't open up?"

"I don't care if you know me or not."

"But we're on the same team now. We should be friends."

"Mind your own business and we'll get along great."

The bear-man smirked when she offered no rejoinder. Round One went to him.

"Is it true you were created in a test tube?"

Exasperation prompted Grizzly to stop and glare. "Keep your nose out of my personal history."

Her features the perfect picture of guileless innocence, Raphaela ignored him. "It must have been terrible being raised as the Doktor's plaything."

"How would you know?" Grizzly snapped, pressing eastward.

"Having no parents is the worst fate anyone can have."

The sadness she'd conveyed caused Grizzly to gaze at her again. Her eyes were averted, her lips curled downward. "Is that the voice of experience speaking?" he asked.

"Yes."

"What happened to your folks?"

"They died when I was six. I hardly remember anything about them," Raphaela disclosed. "But at least I knew them for a short while. I bet it was terrible not having any at all."

"You have no idea," Grizzly said softly. "My earliest memories are of my days at the Biological Center, the Doktor's former headquarters in Cheyenne, Wyoming. All infant genetically engineered hybrids were reared in an enormous nursery from conception to the age of four. After that our schooling began."

"The Doktor provided for your education? How sweet."

"Oh, he provided, all right. In addition to courses in English and the basics we were taught how to kill in a thousand different ways. One of the classes was called *Modern Torture Techniques*. Another was *Humans as a Food Source*. Then there were courses on combat strategy, the psychology of fear, and my personal favorite, *Hybrids: The Superior Race*."

"How horrible."

"Not when you fully appreciate the Doktor's motives. Nearly all of his test-tube offspring were mustered into his personal assassin corps. Our entire education was geared towards making up the most efficient, elite corps of killers ever assembled. We were brainwashed into believing the Doktor cared for us and programmed to obey his every order without delay."

"Yet you rebelled."

"The brainwashing didn't take with all of us. Those possessing exceptionally aggressive natures were the ones who gave the Doktor the most trouble," Grizzly said. "Ask Blade sometime about one of the hybrids living at the Home, a guy named Lynx. The feisty runt actually tried to assassinate the Doktor. Almost succeeded too."

"Do you know him?"

"We were fairly close in the old days," Grizzly stated, and grinned. "I was there the night Lynx tried to rip the Doktor apart. Other hybrids rushed to the madman's aid and managed to capture Lynx, but not before he killed fourteen of them."

"Fourteen? He must be as tough as you are."

"How would you know I'm tough?"

"Blade has told us a little about you. He said you're the best fighter he's ever met."

"Blade did?"

"Yes. This was before he took off after you. I got the impression he missed you very much."

Grizzly made no comment for a while, his throat oddly constricted.

"I'm very, very sorry about Athena," said Raphaela. "She was nice to me when we met."

The bear-man coughed. "I'd rather not bring her up if you don't mind."

"Sorry."

"It's all right. No harm done."

Raphaela promptly changed the subject. "Is it true you think all humans are scum?"

Pausing, the hybrid studied her, surprised there was no malice in her voice or on her countenance. "I did at one time," he admitted. "In another lifetime." He didn't bother to explain that it had been before he met Athena and Blade, when he'd still wrongly believed every human despised his kind. His beloved and the Warrior had taught him otherwise. There were humans who could see past the fur and the claws and recognize the person underneath; there were humans who treated hybrids with the basic respect every being deserved.

Again the breeze changed, blowing harder, stirring the nearby trees.

Grizzly inhaled the sweet scent once more, only this time it was much stronger than previously. He swiveled, striving to ascertain the direction from which the scent came, and concluded the wind was carrying the odor from the east.

"What is it?" Raphaela asked. "Your nose is twitching like crazy."

"I keep picking up this strange scent."

"An animal?"

"No."

"Is it a person then?"

"No. I don't know what it is," Grizzly said, walking slowly while trying to further pinpoint the source of the unusual smell.

Raphaela scanned the verdant forest, smiling when she saw a small bunny hopping into a patch of weeds. "One day I hope to live in a place just like this canyon."

"Don't you intend to return to the Mound?" Grizzly inquired, referring to the immense subterranean city in which the Moles dwelt in north-central Minnesota.

"Never!"

Her passionate declaration brought Grizzly's head around. "Don't you like it there?"

"No," Raphaela said, conveying a fierce intensity in that single word.

"Why not?"

"I don't want to talk about it."

So now the shoe was on the other foot. Perplexed by the Molewoman's vehemence, Grizzly nevertheless chose to drop the subject for the time being.

"I'm happy being on the Force," Raphaela went on rapidly, "and I hope to stay on the team for as long as Blade will have me."

"Your enlistment is only for a year."

"I don't care. I'm sure Wolfe will agree to my staying on."

"Wolfe?"

"The leader of the Moles," Raphaela said softly, almost distastefully.

"You don't sound very fond of him."

"I hate the man."

Grizzly came to a large log and sat down. He was shocked to see moisture welling in her eyes and a crimson tinge to her cheeks. "Why don't we take a break," he offered.

Nodding, Raphaela moved to one side and turned her back to him. Her shoulders bobbed gently.

Now what the hell was this action? Grizzly wondered. The woman was crying! He didn't know what to say. In his estimation her emotional behavior served to confirm his belief that she had no business being in the elite unit. While engaging in a war exercise was hardly the right time to get all choked up over personal problems. She clearly lacked self-control, and anyone who did wouldn't last long on a tactical squad.

A number of sparrows were perched in a nearby tree, singing contentedly. They suddenly stopped.

Grizzly came off the log and looked at them, observing the birds stare eastward and then wing frantically off to the north. Something out there had scared them, driven them off. But what? The mountain lion he'd scented? "Raphaela?"

"What?" she responded, sniffling.

"Snap out of it, girl. There may be something stalking us."

Wiping the back of her left hand across her watery eyes, Raphaela looked around. "Where?"

"That way," Grizzly said, pointing. His sharp ears registered the barely audible patter of furtive movement, of someone or something in the brush 20 yards distant.

"What is it?"

"Don't know yet. Could be a cougar."

"Let's go see."

"No. We'll let it come to us."

A lone person in buckskins abruptly appeared, running toward them, his long hair flying, a heavy spear clutched in his left hand.

"It's Sparrow!" Raphaela declared.

The Flathead swiftly covered the ground. He reached the log and stopped, leaning on it for support and gulping in air, flushed from his exertion. "We were attacked," he gasped breathlessly.

"By who?" Grizzly asked, searching the woods behind the Indian but seeing no sign of pursuit.

"You won't believe me," Sparrow said.

Raphaela came over and reached across the log to grip his shoulder. "We'll believe you. Tell us who did it."

"Blade."

The hybrid and the Molewoman shared amazed looks.

"I told you that you wouldn't believe me," Sparrow said, "but it's the truth. Blade knocked out Lobo, Doc, and me. He dragged the others off. I revived before he could take me and came to find you."

"Blade would never attack any of us," Raphaela stated skeptically. "Are you sure it was him?"

Sparrow Hawk nodded. "I was standing as close to him as I am to you."

"I don't care if you were nose-to-nose. Blade wouldn't do such a thing," Grizzly stated flatly. He gestured at the trees. "Show us where this happened."

"Certainly," Sparrow said, and coughed violently. He braced both hands on the log, the spear resting under each palm. "Just give me a second to catch my breath."

"Hurry," Grizzly urged, shifting to check the terrain to their rear just in case.

In a smooth, quick motion Sparrow Hawk swept the blunt end of the spear up and around, catching the bearman on the back of the head with a resounding smack. Grizzly slumped, his knees sagging, and Sparrow struck him again, then a third time. Soundlessly the hybrid pitched to the turf.

Momentarily stupefied by the assault, Raphaela finally blurted out accusingly, "Sparrow!"

"No," the Flathead said, smirking, and gave her the same treatment.

CHAPTER ELEVEN

"Shouldn't we have seen some sign of the Rangers by now?" Sergeant Havoc said.

"I would have thought so," Blade responded, glancing over his left shoulder at the noncom.

They were on the north bank of the stream, and had traveled over three miles from the mouth of Dutchman Canyon. Other than fish and birds, they'd seen nothing move and found no clues to where the Rangers might be hiding.

"When those guys take up defensive positions they don't fool around," Havoc quipped. "They're better at concealing themselves than Special Forces personnel."

"If there are Rangers here."

"You don't believe there are?"

"Let's just say I'm having my doubts," Blade told him. He studied the thick vegetation bordering the stream, pondering whether to simply call off the exercise on his own initiative and attract the rest of his team by firing several shots into the air.

"The Rangers could be farther up the canyon."

"Could be," Blade admitted, although he didn't believe

they were. "We'll go another mile or so. If we don't find any trace of them by then, we're heading back to the pickup point."

"Are you allowed to do that?"

"I can do whatever I want. The Federation leaders gave me complete autonomy when they appointed me as head of the Force."

"They must regard you very highly, sir," Havoc noted, cradling his M-16 in his arms. "From what I understand, you pretty much have your run of the Federation. And your word is basically law."

"Whenever the safety of the Federation is at stake, I've been empowered to deal with such threats as I see fit," Blade told him. "And I've been granted unlimited authority to enter the territory of any Federation faction."

"And the Outlands?"

"Anywhere a menace arises."

"But the Federation doesn't have legal authority over the Outlands."

"No one does," Blade said, amused that the noncom would quibble over such a minor technicality.

They walked in silence for several minutes.

"In addition to the stories my brother told, I've read about some of your exploits in the papers," Havoc said. "You're considered to be the most important man in the Federation. Some say that without you the Federation would fall apart."

"Nonsense," Blade replied. "There are others who would fill my shoes."

"Like who?"

"Almost any one of the Warriors at the Home is capable of taking charge of the Force. Grizzly could also, despite what he thinks."

"But none of them would have the same influence you do. The leaders of the different factions agreed to give you virtually unlimited power because they know and trust you. They probably wouldn't trust Grizzly or anyone else as much."

The profoundly truthful insight caused the Warrior to nod in agreement. "You're right there," he conceded.

"My brothers were very lucky to serve under you."

Blade didn't respond.

"Tell me about Alaska," Havoc unexpectedly said.

"Alaska?"

"Yes, sir. Jimmy told me you guys barely got out with your lives. Thunder was critically wounded there, wasn't he?"

The painful memories flooded Blade's mind. "Yes," he said softly. "So were Athena and Bear, but they both lived."

"Who was your opposition in Alaska?"

"The Exalted Executioner of the Lords of Kismet," Blade replied, mentally reliving the grueling ordeal. "A woman named Janus Goldmane. She came close to destroying us."

"Did you kill her?"

"She escaped. I expect to hear from her again one of these days."

"Maybe those Lords of Kismet weren't very pleased with her performance and took care of her for you," Havoc speculated.

"I wish," Blade said.

"Who are the Lords of Kismet, by the way?"

"No one knows for certain. We were able to learn that they rule Asia and have established a network of assassins in Europe and Africa. They're experts at fomenting terror and have no scruples whatsoever. From the intelligence we uncovered, they seem to be trying to control the entire world."

Sergeant Havoc laughed. "Quite an ambition."

VENGEANCE STRIKE   107

"The Lords of Kismet aren't the first power-mongers to crave absolute control of the human race and they won't be the last. Eventually the Force will have to take them out."

"It might be easier said than done. If they control Asia they must be extremely powerful."

Blade had often reached the same obvious conclusion. Taking the Lords of Kismet on would be the ultimate challenge. He couldn't do it with the current team, not unless they improved drastically. Even if they did, the logistics of getting the Force to Asia and back were daunting.

The stream curved to the south, widening slightly. Foam swirled around a large rock jutting above the surface.

As the Warrior advanced he pondered the reason for the exercise charade. What motive did Gallagher have in sending the Force out on phony maneuvers? Initially he'd suspected that the Rangers would be a special group handpicked by the general and under orders to slay the team. Not finding any Rangers at all was totally unexpected, especially since Gallagher had gone to all the trouble to have Lieutenant Wharton greet them and explain the bogus rules.

Very strange.

Blade concluded that the general's main purpose had been to strand the Force in Dutchman Canyon. But why? There had to be a logical reason. He wouldn't put it past the wily fox to have professional killers stationed at strategic intervals, but so far there had been no enemy action.

Another, more disturbing, possibility occured to him. What if Gallagher had wanted to get the team away from the Force Facility? Although he couldn't fathom any conceivable motive for such a tactic, it was plausible. If so, he'd played right into the officer's hands.

Blade hoped the others were faring okay. He'd heard no gunshots, which in itself proved nothing but tended to reassure him that they were having no better luck than he was. Repeatedly he gazed to the north and south, attempting to spot them.

"You must miss your family a lot."

The unusual comment made Blade look at the noncom, who grinned. "Yes, I do."

"How often do you get back to the Home to see them?"

"Not often enough."

"Didn't your wife and son live in Los Angeles for a while?"

"Yeah, but they weren't happy there."

"I don't blame them, sir. L.A. is like a jungle where only the strong survive."

Now why did Havoc bring them up? Blade asked himself. For that matter, the soldier was doing entirely too much talking for a member of Special Forces. Havoc should know better than to gab while on patrol. Neither of the other Havocs would have committed such a blatant breach of discipline. Surely the staff sergeant had received comprehensive training in . . .

Other Havocs?

Dear Spirit!

The chilling insight hit him with all the force of a sledgehammer, causing him to stop short in bewilderment. It couldn't be! he told himself. And yet . . . and yet there was no denying Steve Havoc had made the statement.

"Is something wrong?" the noncom asked.

"No," Blade responded, shaking his head, and resumed hiking along the stream. He must be careful not to alert Havoc to his sudden suspicion. Perhaps it was unwarranted. Maybe there was a perfectly valid reason for the noncom's mistake.

No.

VENGEANCE STRIKE   109

There couldn't be.

His mind in turmoil, Blade scarcely paid attention to his surroundings as he attempted to cope with the profoundly disturbing implications. He reviewed the sequence of events from the moment of his return to the present, seeing everything in a brand-new light. The insight explained so much.

It explained why General Gallagher had accepted Steve Havoc on the Force at the spur of the moment.

It explained why Havoc had tried to "save" the little girl.

It explained why the noncom failed to adhere to proper military protocol as had his brothers, as would any member of the Special Forces.

It explained why there were no Rangers anywhere in Dutchman Canyon.

There were aspects still unresolved, but now Blade knew how to get the answers. He halted several yards past the curve and turned.

Sergeant Havoc took one look at the giant's face and stopped in mid-stride. A lopsided grin curved his lips. "I goofed somewhere, didn't I?"

Blade held the M-16 at waist height, the barrel slanted toward the ground. Confident in his prowess, he didn't bother to cover the young man.

"I see it in your eyes," Havoc went on in an unconcerned fashion, his own rifle tucked in the crook of his left arm and angled downward.

"You're very perceptive," Blade stated.

"My kind is adept at reading human expressions. You might say that we're students of mortal physiology."

"Your kind?"

Not bothering to explain, Havoc pressed his own question. "Where did I screw up?"

"You claimed that your brother Jim told you about our

mission in Alaska."

"Yeah? So?"

"So Jim Havoc died in Canada en route back from Alaska to L.A. He couldn't have related our encounter with Janus Goldmane."

"Damn," Havoc said, and chuckled. "And here I thought I was doing so well."

"You're not a Havoc, are you?"

"Nope," the noncom bluntly admitted smiling. "There is a real Steve Havoc and he is in Special Forces. I've seen him once, but I'm not him."

"You assumed his identity to get onto the Force."

"Sure did," the imposter said, moving to a boulder a few feet to the left on which he took a seat. He leaned his M-16 against it.

"Did General Gallagher put you up to it?"

The young man shook his head.

"I find that hard to accept."

"Only because you don't know as much as you think you know," the imposter stated, smirking.

"I know that you've never been attached to Special Forces, and I have my doubts that you have any military experience at all."

"Give the man a prize."

"And I know that you tried to save that girl, or whatever she was, to legitimize your false identity, to demonstrate to all of us that you have the qualities of a good soldier."

"Yes and no," the fake said, and laughed.

"What *was* she, by the way? How did she climb over the electrified fence?"

"All in good time."

Blade took a step toward him. "What's your real name?"

"It would hardly interest you."

"Try me."

"My real name was bestowed so long ago that occasionally I forget what it is," declared the fake Havoc wistfully. "After assuming so many identities over the years, I guess such a lapse is only natural."

"You've done this before?"

A sigh and a nod preceded the answer. "More times than all the minutes you have lived."

"That's impossible," Blade stated. He assumed the man must be stalling for some reason, and became annoyed. "Quit playing games. You still haven't told me your name."

"Very well. I am Zhongli Quan."

The Warrior took another stride. "That's funny. You don't look Oriental."

"How perceptive," Quan said.

"Quit with the fairy tales. What's your true name?"

"I'm Zhongli Quan," the man insisted. "I was born in Sinkiang in the year 1068, which ranks me as one of the oldest living creatures on this paltry planet. I have done all there is to do and seen all there is to see. Once my kind were numerous and we held many important positions of leadership, exploiting humans as we saw fit. But that was before the truth about our nature became known to the ancients and they waged an effective campaign to exterminate every last one of us." He paused, concluding sadly, "Now there are very few Gualaons left."

"What *are* you babbling about?"

"Do you know who Genghis Khan was?"

Blade nodded, definitely convinced the guy was deliberately buying time. But why? Were his cohorts on the way?

"Many historians have rightly wondered how the chief of a small Mongol tribe went on to control one of the largest empires ever established," Quan said matter-offactly, in the manner of a history teacher addressing a student. "They've been mystified by the Khan's repeated victories over vastly more powerful and skilled armies. Of course, they've categorically denied the historical records that speak of the great Khan's receiving supernatural aid. But he did, you see. He enlisted our assistance."

"You're nuts," Blade stated, stepping up to the bogus noncom. "And I'm tired of your stalling tactics. We're going to go find the rest of the team and take you back to the Force Facility. Then I'll call Gallagher and have him pick you up. I don't know what little scheme the two of you concocted, but it's over as of this minute."

"My dear Warrior, it's just beginning."

Blade saw the blow coming, saw the man's right fist flash toward his jaw, and he started to evade the punch, to dodge to one side. He hadn't felt the man posed any serious threat since the much smaller pretender could hardly hope to match his prodigious strength and ruggedness. So he was all the more surprised when the noncom's knuckles connected with the tip of his jaw and the blow lifted him from his feet and sent him sailing rearward over a yard. He crashed onto his back, the world spinning above him, and feebly pushed into a sitting position. The M-16 lay a foot away and it might as well have been a mile.

Zhongli Quan slid from the boulder and straightened, a peculiar melancholy etching his face. "You're too overconfident for your own good."

The Warrior wasn't about to agree. He rose unsteadily, his hands dropping to his Bowies.

"They won't save you now," Quan said, and gazed past the giant. "Are the rest taken care of, Zhang?"

Blade thought the man was resorting to the oldest trick in the book until someone spoke directly behind him.

VENGEANCE STRIKE

"They were child's play."

"Then do the honors with this fool."

Starting to draw his knifes, Blade tried to spin, to confront this new threat. But a tremendous blow seemed to cave in his head and an inky veil shrouded his mind.

CHAPTER TWELVE

The Warrior awoke, surprised to be alive and seated on a hard surface with his back propped against something equally hard. He felt a breeze on his face and realized his wrists and ankles were tightly bound, his hands resting between his legs. Pain lanced all his limbs. He opened his eyes a crack, not knowing what to expect but certainly not expecting to see other trussed legs near his own. Slowly twisting his neck, he saw Raphaela and Grizzly on his right and Doc, Lobo, and Sparrow on his left. All were unconscious.

"You're awake already?"

Blade saw a pair of combat boots walk into his limited field of vision and halt in front of him. Since feigning unconsciousness was now out of the question, he opened his eyes wide and gazed into the grinning face of Zhongli Quan.

"My compliments, Warrior," said his captor. "You were the last taken. By all rights you should be out for another two or three hours. Your recuperative powers are amazing."

VENGEANCE STRIKE

"What are you up to now?" Blade asked. "Why are you doing this?"

"An explanation will be forthcoming shortly," Quan stated, and turned to stare into the distance.

The Warrior checked his surroundings. He and his companions had been placed in a natural stone amphitheater, the open end facing due east. A low, smooth wall, the very wall against which he and the others had been placed, partially enclosed a stone floor 15 feet in diameter. Overhead were a few fluffy cumulous clouds and the sun, the fiery orb hanging just shy of the midday position. Glancing toward the opening he saw a pile of weapons a yard from it, and among them were his Bowies.

Quan was intently scouring the forest beyond.

"Where's your buddy?" Blade asked, as much in the hope of learning important information as of keeping the man distracted. He still had his ace in the hole, and when the time came he didn't want Quan to have any forewarning.

"He went to the mouth of the canyon to confirm there are no military personnel in the area. Different branches use Dutchman for training purposes. Although no legitimate war games are scheduled for three more days, every now and then an officer will bring a squad out here on his own initiative. We can't afford to take any chances. Our kind must be extremely cautious or we'll all perish," Quan said, and grinned. "Besides, we don't want to be disturbed once we begin."

"Begin what?"

"You'll see."

"Did General Gallagher hire the two of you?"

The noncom glanced at the giant and frowned. "You still don't comprehend the truth. And here I was led to believe that you're extremely intelligent—for a human."

"There you go again, talking as if you're not."

The phony soldier glanced at the giant. "I expected better from you. Your reputation is highly overrated."

"I squeak by."

"Not this time."

A low groan heralded Grizzly's revival. His eyes snapped wide and he glared about until he saw Raphaela and Blade. Then he focused on Quan. "What the hell is going on, Havoc?" he demanded, lifting his arms. "Somebody will pay for this."

"Sparrow Hawk, perhaps?" Quan said sarcastically, and pointed at the unconscious Flathead.

The man-beast leaned forward and became aware of the three other insensate Force members. "Sparrow! But he's the one who knocked me out."

"Did he indeed?" Quan responded, capping his mocking tone with a brittle laugh.

"I don't get any of this," Grizzly said, looking at the Warrior. "What's happening?"

"Your guess is as good as mine," Blade told him.

"Who nailed you?"

Blade nodded at Quan.

"Him?" Grizzly declared. "Did he clobber you when you weren't looking?"

"I wish. He's much stronger than he seems."

"If I ever get my hands free the sucker is history," Grizzly vowed, squaring his shoulders and straining his wrists against the rope biting into his flesh.

Instantly Quan moved over to the hybrid and cuffed him across the face, splitting Grizzly's left cheek open. The bear-man sagged, but only momentarily, and when he recovered, his eyes blazed savage hatred.

"Make no attempt to escape," Quan warned, "or I'll tear your head from your shoulders, orders or no orders."

Seeing Grizzly's body tense as if the hybrid were about

VENGEANCE STRIKE 117

to try and spring upward, Blade intervened to take the heat off his friend. "So you *are* working for someone else. I thought so."

Quan swung around. "But not who you think it is."

Out of the corner of his eye Blade saw someone entering the amphitheater. He looked, and promptly experienced an upwelling of red hot rage.

Strolling closer, smiling happily, was the bulldog himself, General Miles Gallagher in full-dress uniform. He halted near the Warrior and chuckled. "I trust you know this means you've failed the exercise."

Blade lost his self-control and attempted to shove to his feet. The officer stepped forward, touched the first finger of his right hand to the Warrior's forehead, and gave a slight shove. To Blade's astonishment, he was slammed back against the wall.

"Behave yourself," Gallagher stated. "Your time will come soon enough."

Quan pointed at the bear-man. "This one was giving me trouble."

"The sooner we get this over with, the better," Gallagher said.

"Are there any humans in the area, Zhang?"

"None. I went as far as the parking area to be doubly certain. We have Dutchman Canyon all to ourselves."

"Excellent," Quan said, smiling. "Then we need not worry about the screams being heard."

Listening to the conversation in confusion, Blade stared from the phony Havoc to General Miles Gallagher and deduced the obvious. "You're not the general," he said to the man called Zhang.

"Thank goodness," Zhang said. He chuckled and moved over to gently poke his elbow into his companion's ribs. "He hasn't figured it out yet, has he?"

"No," Quan said, equally amused. "And now that I

think about it, we shouldn't hold it against him. There haven't been any Gualaons in North America since the Salem trials. His ignorance is excusable."

Blade's brow knit as he attempted to fit the pieces of the puzzle together. "Are you referring to the witch trials in Salem, Massachusetts, way back in the 1690's?"

"Yes," Quan said, and winked at Zhang. "See? He's not a complete moron, which is more than we can say about the majority of his kind."

"One of our cousins caused all the trouble in Salem," Zhang told the giant. "Tituba started the hysteria as sort of a prank. With her ability to transform she easily convinced a few local girls that she was a witch, and tricked them into engaging in harmless witchcraft rituals. But it got out of control. The girls were found out, and to cover themselves started accusing everyone they disliked of being in league with the Devil. A court of inquiry was established, and by the time self-righteous Cotton Mather and his inquisitors were done, thirteen women and six men, all innocent of any wrongdoing, had been put to death."

"Tituba never did know when to keep her big mouth shut," commented Quan.

Blade felt a tingle run down his spine. The sincerity with which the pair made their disclosure spurred a startling realization. They were telling the *truth*. As with Quan's comments about Genghis Khan, the duo had honestly related simple history. Which meant they must be millennia old. "What *are* you?" he inquired.

"At last," Quan said, laughing.

Grizzly was looking at the Warrior. "Will you tell me what this is all about? Are these guys nut cases?"

"No," Blade said. He scrutinized the fake Gallagher. "Where is the real general?"

"Dead."

VENGEANCE STRIKE

The Warrior leaned back against the stone wall. Suddenly everything came into perspective. "How long?" he asked softly.

"About a year," Zhang answered. "I was assigned to take his place right after you destroyed our Masters' operation in Alaska."

"Your Masters?" Blade repeated, stunned.

"I don't get any of this," Grizzly snapped, glaring at the noncom and the officer. "I was there in Alaska. We took on some bimbo who worked for the Lords of Kismet. Are you telling us that you two clowns work for them?"

"Another brilliant mind," Quan said scornfully.

"The High Lords were most displeased when you ruined their scheme to destroy California and ultimately the rest of the Freedom Federation," Zhang detailed. "They decided to eliminate the Force before making another such attempt, and to do so in a manner that wouldn't arouse any suspicion whatsoever."

"From within," Blade said, emotionally reeling from the shattering revelation.

"Yes," Zhang said. "I was transported across the Pacific and entered Los Angeles the day after Goldmane failed. Killing Gallagher and assuming his identity was ridiculously easy." He glanced at the bear-man. "It was I who persuaded your former lover to fake her own death."

"You!" Grizzly exclaimed, his features hardening.

Zhang nodded, enjoying himself. "I've tried every trick I could think of to get the Force to slit its own throat. Had I succeeded, none of us would be here right now."

"Wait a minute," Blade said, his mind awhirl. "There are some things I don't understand. How did you cross the Pacific? By plane?"

"That you will never know. It's classified," Zhang replied.

"Okay. Then explain something else. Why did you assume General Gallagher's identity? Why not become the governor? Or why not become one of the team?"

"Because the intelligence provided by the Lords' agents in California indicated Gallagher was ideal for our Masters' purposes. He dealt with your unit on a daily basis. The governor, however, rarely has any personal dealings with the Force," Zhang related. "As for becoming one of the team, that was considered too risky. Hybrids have heightened senses and might have detected the subterfuge."

Blade absently gazed at Grizzly and saw unbridled rage reflected on the man-beast's face.

"Actually, I thought I had succeeded at my mission," Zhang said reflectively. "You disbanded the unit after the Canadian episode and I sent word to the Lords that my job was done." He paused. "But they were so pleased with my work, they ordered me to continue impersonating Gallagher and learn all I could about the Free State of California, everything of military and scientific importance, every weakness that could be exploited at a future date."

Quan nodded, staring at the giant. "And then you surprised us by reforming the unit."

"The Lords were most unhappy to hear the news," Zhang said. "Again I tried to bring about the team's downfall, only this time you were too smart for me."

"And since the Lords of Kismet have another important plan in the works, and they don't want the Force interfering, we were instructed to terminate all of you," Quan concluded. "Luring you here under the pretext of a combat exercise was our own idea. Pretty clever, eh?"

Blade gazed at the smug duo, dazed. Never in his wildest imaginings would he have suspected the truth. "What's your part in this?" he asked the false noncom.

"I'm Zhang's partner. Had something happened to him, I was ready to take his place or do whatever might be needed to accomplish our assignment. I also handle whatever other impersonations are needed," Quan said, and added, "The mighty Lords always dispatch Gualaons in pairs."

Blade had a thought. "Is the real Steve Havoc dead?"

"No," Quan answered. "His squad was sent to the border before I could dispose of him."

"Why did you chose to impersonate him?"

"Originally I intended to convince his brother to help Zhang, alias Gallagher, destroy the Force. But when Grizzly and you returned from the Outlands alone, we decided to change our plans and install me on the Force as Mike Havoc's replacement. We knew we were taking a risk of being discovered by the hybrids, but we wanted an inside man to keep an eye on you until our plan was put into effect."

"And to keep us off balance you had that little girl, or whatever she was, pay us a visit. Then one of you painted the verse on the supply bunker," Blade said.

"We wanted you so confused that you didn't know which way was up," Quan confirmed. "It made our job easier."

"And the reason for impersonating Jaguarundi?"

"Was twofold. First, we wanted to make all of you suspicious of each other."

"Except for Havoc," Blade corrected him. "That's why you pretended to save the girl from the fence. You wanted me to believe he was dependable."

"Yes. Little did we know you would reprimand him."

"And what about the second reason for impersonating Jag?"

"We wanted one of the hybrids out of the way for today. Combined they might have presented a problem. Since the cat-man is somewhat more intelligent than Grizzly and his feline reflexes a shade sharper, not to mention his great speed, we decided to cast a shadow of doubt on his loyalty,'' Quan detailed. He nodded at the bear-man. "This oaf was no threat to us."

To Blade's surprise the hybrid didn't respond. Grizzly sat with his eyes closed, his lips compressed.

"Now we will dispose of all of you and be back in L.A. by nightfall," Zhang commented.

"Don't you think Governor Melnick will be the least bit suspicious when we simply disappear off the face of the earth?" Blade asked.

"Not at all," Zhang said. "You see, in my guise as General Gallagher I'll go to the governor and sadly report that all of you were slain by a traitor in your midst while engaged in a field exercise in Dutchman Canyon."

"Let me guess," Blade said. "The traitor will be Jag."

Zhang beamed. "You learn quickly."

"And since the incident in my office is already a matter of record, it will be impossible for Jag to convince anyone of his innocence," Blade concluded.

"The perfect crime,' Quan boasted. "All six of you will be dead, Jag will either be arrested or flee California, and the Force will be finished. Our Lords can carry out their plans without fear of being checkmated again. All's well that ends well."

Blade couldn't dispute the brilliance of their demented plot. But one question remained. "You didn't answer me earlier. What are you? How are you able to impersonate someone so completely?"

"Our kind has existed on this sphere since the dawn of time. When humans first appeared, we thought nothing of it. The early Gualaons regarded mortals as little better than animals. For centuries the two races co-existed in peace. But since humans breed like rabbits, your race quickly outnumbered ours. Later, your kind came to distrust and fear us. Eventually, they wiped most of us out."

"Why did the ancients grow to fear your kind if the Gualaons meant them no harm?"

"Simply because of our inherent ability, one not much different than that of the chameleon. But where those quaint reptiles merely change color, we do much more."

"Show me."

"Why not?" Zhang responded. "You can take the truth with you into our bellies."

Blade glanced at his friends. Doc was beginning to stir, but the rest were still unconscious. He had to stall as long as possible. "Gualaons eat humans?"

"We eat all lower life-forms, although my kind didn't start consuming humans on a regular basis until after your ancestors turned on us," Quan said. He motioned to Zhang. "Why don't you perform the demonstration?"

"Gladly," the other said, and stepped back a few steps. He smiled benignly at the Warrior, lowered his arms to his sides, and relaxed.

Not knowing what to expect, Blade watched in fascination commingled with incipient horror as the man's face started to shift, to change, as if the very skin were melting, the chin becoming rounded, the nose thinner, the eyes slanted and green. A pale fluid poured from Zhang's pores, flowing downward, rapidly soaking his uniform, and the clothes began to change as well. It all transpired so fast Blade could scarcely credit his eyes.

Quan gazed at his fellow being in transparent envy. "Actually, I didn't quite tell you everything. Our kind has become addicted to human flesh over the centuries. It's our primary food source now. If we try to go without it we suffer a form of withdrawal. The Lords have developed a drug that helps to stem our hunger, but not indefinitely. You have no idea how much we are going to enjoy gorging on two or three of you. The rest we must regretfully leave intact for the authorities to examine."

A sweet stench assailted Blade's nostrils. He saw reddish hair sprout all over the creature known as Zhang, saw a black loincloth materialize about the waist, and guessed the end result of the transformation. The fingernails on Zhang/Gallagher's hand grew an inch in less than a minute, solidifying into tapered claws. The eyes acquired distinctive vertical slits. Both ears acquired a feline aspect.

"I wish you could see your face," Quan said, and chortled in triumph.

"He's becoming Jag."

Quan nodded. "You don't miss a trick, do you? Since we want Jag to take the blame, it's only fitting for Jag to do the killing." He snickered and clapped his hands in delight.

Mesmerized, the Warrior witnessed the conclusion of the astounding metamorphosis. Where previously there had stood a robust, normal human, one of the highest-ranking officers in the California military, there now stood the genetically engineered hybrid named Jaguarundi.

"Your people have had many names for us down through the ages and portrayed us in different ways," Quan related. "Cro-Magnons painted us on their cave walls. Africans have called us galadina, hyena-men and leopard-men and jackal-men. In Burma we are called Taws. In Japan, tanuki. In Germany we were branded as werewolves. Psychologists before the war liked to refer to a presumed delusion dubbed lycanthropy to explain our kind. But in all countries, among all the races of men, these names all refer to the trait that most distinguishes us from humans. That is why, first and last, we are regarded by your people as *shapeshifters.*"

"How did you acquire this ability?" Blade asked, observing the fake Jag sniff the air and smirk.

"Haven't you been listening?" Quan rejoined. "We have always been this way. We are Gualaons."

"But where did you come from?"

"The origin of our people is lost in antiquity. Our ancestors had a legend that we came from the stars, but that's ridiculous."

The creature resembling Jag made an impatient gesture. "Enough talk, Quan. I'm hungry. Let's eat."

"Be my guest."

Zhang took a step toward the Warrior. "I think we'll start with you. There's enough meat on you to fill both of us."

A new voice intruded on the scene, coming from the direction of the ampitheater's opening. "Not so fast there, Chuckles. If you eat him you're bound to get indigestion."

Both shapeshifters swung toward the source.

At last! Blade wanted to shout, relief coursing through him as he looked at his ace in the hole.

Leaning nonchalantly against the stone wall, his fur caked with perspiration, was the real Jaguarundi.

CHAPTER THIRTEEN

Both shapeshifters sprang toward the cat-man and Jag crouched, prepared to meet their rush head-on until he glanced at Blade and saw the Warrior give a sharp shake of his head. Obediently he wheeled and raced into the forest. He didn't know why the giant didn't want him to take them on then and there, but he'd learned to implicitly trust Blade during the half year or so they'd been working together, and reasoned that the Warrior must have a good reason.

A look over his right shoulder revealed that the creature resembling him was still in pursuit, but the other one had stopped at the edge of the amphitheater and was turning back. Perhaps Blade had hoped he would draw both of them off, giving the Force members time to free themselves. If so, he'd only partially succeeded.

What *were* those things? Jag wondered. He'd arrived on the scene just as a man who had looked every bit like General Gallagher had unexpectedly transformed into a carbon copy of himself. The spectacle had stunned him. Unable to hear much of the conversation between Blade and the pair, he knew nothing about the opposition.

A few assumptions, though, were obvious. The creature chasing him, or perhaps the other shapeshifter, had impersonated him at the Facility and attacked Blade, probably in the hope that Blade would have Jag locked up and throw away the key. Which only proved how little they knew the Warrior. A less intelligent, less imaginative man might have accepted the bogus attack at its face value, but Blade had wisely pierced the facade.

The day before, when Jag had entered the giant's office as requested after being placed under house arrest, Blade had immediately apologized for doing so and explained that it had been a ruse designed to convince whoever was behind the attack to mistakenly think their plan had worked. Blade had told Jag that never for a minute did he think Jag was responsible. And he'd given Jag new orders, asserting that Jag had become his ace in the hole. Since their enemies believed Jag to be under arrest, they wouldn't be expecting the ploy Blade concocted.

Jag grinned as he ran. He had to hand it to the Warrior; the man seldom missed a trick. Blade had instructed him to follow the convoy truck at a discreet distance, to trail it all the way to Dutchman Canyon, relying on Jag's exceptional speed and endurance to achieve a feat no other human or hybrid could possibly perform.

It had been a close call.

Even though the truck seldom drove over 50, keeping it in sight had taxed Jag to new limits and beyond. He'd never covered so many miles at one stretch, and never run for 90 minutes while averaging 25 to 30 miles an hour the entire distance. Small wonder, then, that he'd been on his last legs when he finally got to Dutchman Canyon, and had needed time to rest before actually entering the canyon to search for his friends. He'd still been hunting for them when he'd spied General Gallagher returning from the parking area and shadowed the man.

And now—surprise, surprise! Not only had it not been the general; it wasn't even human!

A loud crackling noise made by his pursuer in the dense brush to his rear shattered Jaguarundi's reflection and brought him to the present, to wrestling with the problem of how to deal with the creature. He wasn't particularly worried. His uncanny reflexes, his supreme quickness, had enabled him to triumph over varied foes in the past. Mutations, humans, and fierce animals had all fallen when pitted against his hybrid abilities. And he felt confident this strange creature would be no different.

Jag angled toward the high south wall of the canyon, toward an immense thicket near its base where he could lose the phony, then circle around and dispatch him. He casually twisted his head to see how much of a lead he had, and received the shock of his life when he beheld his grim-faced antagonist not 12 feet behind him.

The guy could run!

Perturbed, Jag poured on the speed, bounding through the woods faster than a fleeing deer, more powerfully than a charging boar, and leaping higher with each stride than the hardiest jackrabbit.

A chilling realization almost made him stumble. What if the thing not only looked like him, but had his ability as well? He'd assumed the transformation involved more surface changes, that it was an alteration in appearance only—skin deep, so to speak. It had never occurred to him that the thing *became* whatever it wanted to become. He hadn't counted on it acquiring his total identity, speed and all.

This meant they were evenly matched.

Jag frowned, skirting a tree and checking on the progress of his eerie twin, who had gained a foot. No, they weren't evenly matched because he was fatigued from following the convoy truck and the creature wasn't even breathing hard. And the longer the pursuit lasted the weaker he would become. He must do something soon, while he still had the strength.

Think! he chided himself.

Think! Think! Think!

Thirty feet ahead reared an oak tree, its lowest limbs not much over seven feet above the ground.

Inspiration struck when Jag glanced at the limb directly in his path. If he timed it properly, he'd take the phony down with a minimum of hassle. But to carry it off he must let the creature get a little closer. Without trying to be too transparent, he slowed slightly, pretending his weariness was getting the better of him.

Another glance showed the shapeshifter eight feet away.

Jag faced front and grinned. Would Blade be pleasantly surprised when he returned with the thing slung across his shoulder! It would justify the Warrior's confidence in him.

The tree was much nearer.

Focusing on the limb, Jag tensed for the leap he must make. All the hours he had spent on the high bar and parallel bars were about to pay off. During his teen years, when the Doktor had required all of his scientifically bred offspring to workout daily in a gym located in the Biological Center to enhance their conditioning, he'd always enjoyed gymnastics. He'd been one of the best, one of the Doktor's favorites, and had been selected to put on exhibitions at banquets for visiting dignitaries.

He carefully gauged the distance, and when only two strides from the oak he launched himself into the air, his arms outstretched, his hands curling around the lowest limb as he swept his legs up and under it. In a flashing arc he swung completely around the branch and speared his legs at the charging imposter. He twisted as he lanced downward, his body rigid and tight, expecting to slam the creature to the ground.

Instead, he missed.

The shapeshifter hadn't fallen for the trick. He'd stopped on a dime, and now threw himself to the right as the cat-man's feet drove at his chest.

Jag had miscalculated terribly, leaving no room for error and having no contingency in case he should fail. Consequently he was unable to recover in time, to abort his attack before he sailed within striking range. His body was three feet off the earth when the shapeshifter lashed out, clipping him in the temple with a backhanded blow. Incredibly, the punch sent Jag tumbling head over heels to crash onto a small boulder.

Exquisite pain bombarded Jag's chest and he doubled over, on his right side on the ground. Dimly he sensed the creature striding over. Firm hands roughly seized him by the shoulders and rudely hauled him upright, where he gazed at his mirror image, a smirking, sinister image that mocked him in its triumph.

"Did you really believe I would fall for such a pathetically simpleminded deception, hybrid?" the shapeshifter asked. "I who have lived more years than a thousand mortals combined?"

Jag couldn't have answered if he wanted to. His ribs were aflame with torment.

"Your kind is dumb as the lowly humans," the shapeshifter declared scornfully, "although they enjoy the distinction of being tastier."

Balling his right fist, Jag tried to pound the creature in the face.

The shapeshifter hissed and suddenly tossed the cat-man through the air as effortlessly as it might an infant.

Jag tried to right himself. Like most felines, he enjoyed an instinctive flair for alighting on his feet whenever he fell from any height. This time his agility failed him.

Swamped by torturing pain, suspecting one or more of his ribs might be cracked, Jag landed off balance, tripped, and fell onto his back.

In a twinkling the shapeshifter stood above the hybrid and grinned. "I understand that you think you're hot stuff when compared to mortals. To me, catling, you're less than nothing."

"Screw you," Jag snapped.

Bending, the shapeshifter seized the hybrid and lifted him overhead. "I guess you need a demonstration."

Jag struggled to break free but the fingers digging into his flesh were solid iron. He winced as the creature swung its arms, then hurled him at the trunk of a tree. His spine took the brunt of the impact and he landed on the grass with his senses swimming. Both his arms and legs were tingling and wouldn't respond to his mental commands. Floating out of a murky space overhead came a taunting voice.

"I can keep this up all day and all night. You see, hybrid, there's something you don't know, the reason you can never defeat me. I'm naturally four times as strong as you are."

A harsh cackle accented the claim.

"When my kind transform, we always retain our inherent personality, intelligence, and strength. So no matter what shape we take, whether that of an adult or, say, a little blond girl, we always possess superhuman power. Mortals and hybrids are no match for us."

Jag wanted to smash in its ugly face but his hands wouldn't acknowledge his brain.

"And as you no doubt noticed at the Facility, our resilient forms can't be harmed by electricity. We're impervious to fire. Bullets can't harm us either unless they strike a vital organ, which is easier said than done because our organs aren't in the same places yours are."

Feeling began to return to Jag's fingers. Keep talking, bastard, he thought, hoping for a chance to nail the thing.

"By now Zhongli should have finished off a few of your buddies," the shapeshifter said. "So I'd better wrap this up or he'll eat all the choice parts himself."

Choice parts? The words echoed in Jag's mind at the precise second his vision cleared and he saw the shapeshifter standing above him. Within arm's reach were the creature's own choice parts, or the junction where they should be, and Jag hoped that at least this set of organs was authentic. He promptly flicked his right fist up and in, scoring hard, his knuckles mashing against a spongy mound.

The creature screeched and desperately retreated, doubling over to clutch at his groin.

Bingo! Jag shoved to his feet, his knees threatening to buckle, and moved in, delivering a left cross that staggered his foe. He still felt weak, too weak for sustained combat, too weak to finish what he'd started. His best bet lay in finding a hiding place to recuperate. With that in mind he spun and plunged into the woods.

"I'll kill you!" came the strangled vow of vengeance from the shapefinder.

You'll have to catch me first, Jag thought, gaining speed with every stride. Putting as much distance as possible between them was the only way of saving his life. He forced his legs to move, his arms to swing in rhythmic motion.

A bellow of rabid rage attended his flight.

Jag went 20 yards, than 30. He looked back and glimpsed the imposter giving chase. Ducking low, he darted behind a short pine tree and dropped prone in the waist-high bushes to its rear. Had the thing seen him? If so, he wouldn't be able to offer much resistance. He held

VENGEANCE STRIKE

his breath, listening, and soon heard the pattering feet of the shapeshifter.

A loud snarl sounded at the very moment the creature drew abreast of Jag's hiding spot, a snarl he supposed meant the thing knew exactly where he was, and he tried to push erect to meet its anticipated attack. But the shapeshifter kept going, bounding off into the undergrowth. Its footfalls grew fainter and fainter, fading to silence.

He'd done it!

Elated, Jag stood and headed toward the amphitheater as rapidly as he could. His friends were in dire jeopardy. They might even be dead. If so, he'd get revenge or perish in the attempt.

Jag's whole body ached and throbbed. In all his travels he'd only met a few who were stronger than he was, the majority hybrids. Blade was an exception, a human endowed with the strength of a colossus. Yet the giant's might would be just a petty annoyance to one of those shapeshifters.

He halted to take his bearings, disoriented by the beating he'd taken and the pain lancing his chest. Satisfied he had picked the right direction, he pressed onward.

The fight with the creature had reemphasized a fundamental point he'd almost forgotten: Never underestimate a foe, no matter what their appearance might be. In this instance the adage was doubly appropriate.

Jag threaded his way among the trees and brush, impatient to get there, thinking about Grizzly possibly being dead. To lose the companionship of his own kind after being alone for so long would be heartbreaking, especially the companionship of one of his few true friends.

Preoccupied with such contemplation, Jag sprinted into a small clearing, and was halfway across before he spotted the figure waiting for him on the other side, a figure he knew as well as he knew his own. Because, externally at least, it was his own.

Grinning wickedly, devilishly impudent in its stance and bearing, its gleaming teeth exposed, was the shapeshifter.

CHAPTER FOURTEEN

Blade went into motion the moment the pair of shapeshifters started after Jaguarundi. He curled his legs underneath him and shoved to his knees, then began to exert his prodigious sinews against the rope binding his wrists. A glance at Grizzly showed the bear-man's eyes were still closed. "Grizzly!" he declared. "Now's our chance to get loose."

Defying all logic, the hybrid didn't respond, didn't budge at all.

"Grizzly!" Blade snapped, and looked eastward.

Jag was leading Zhang into the forest, but Guan had turned and was on his way back into the amphitheater.

Too soon! Blade realized, surging against the rope until his face became livid and his veins bulged. He ignored the approaching creature, hoping he could part the rope before the thing reached him, but a brittle laugh almost at his left elbow alerted him otherwise.

"Nice try, Warrior."

A combat boot slammed into Blade's shoulder, knocking him into his back. He stared up into the imitation features of Sergeant Steve Havoc.

"I suppose the cat-man happened to be out jogging and accidentally stumbled on this place?"

Blade didn't reply. His legs were bent to the right, his knees a yard from the shapeshifter. He tensed his muscles in preparation for making his move.

"It appears you possess more intellect than we gave you credit for," Quan said in admiration. "Or did you merely change your mind about putting Jaguarundi under house arrest?"

"He never really was," Blade elaborated, wishing the creature would take a step or two nearer. He didn't want to risk missing.

"And here we thought we were being so clever. Where did we go wrong?"

"Jag would never attack me. I knew there had to be another explanation, but I never came close to suspecting the truth."

"So let me guess," Quan said. "You instructed him to trail the convoy truck?"

The Warrior nodded, primed and ready.

"For a human you're rather devious," the shapeshifter stated, his hands on his hips. "But no matter. Now we'll simply kill Jag too and make it appear that a wild mutation was responsible for all of your deaths."

"There's bound to be a formal inquiry."

"So?" Quan said, shrugging. "All the evidence will implicate a feral brute. No one will ever suspect General Miles Gallagher and Sergeant Steve Havoc."

"The real Havoc will catch on."

"He's history the minute his squad returns from the border."

"You have it all figured out."

Quan chuckled. "I try."

"The Lords of Kismet must be very proud of their murderous, bloodthirsty slaves," Blade stated, intentionally attempting to provoke his foe.

"We're not slaves, fool," Quan declared irately. "We are members of the High Assassin Corps of Lord Shiva."

"Who?"

"Shiva the Destroyer, one of the Lords of Kismet, one of the three most powerful beings in Asia."

Fascinated at gleaning insights into the workings of the Oriental hierarchy, Blade probed deeper. "Beings? Are the Lords mutations of some kind?"

"In a sense."

"But you look down your nose at Jag and Grizzly and they're both mutations. How can you serve beings you rate as inferior?"

"The Lords of Kismet are much more than ordinary hybrids. They are the first and the last, the be-all and end-all. They know all things and wield all power."

"If they're so powerful, why don't they try to destroy the Force themselves?"

"You can't expect them to deal with every petty problem personally," Quan said. He cocked his head and pursed his lips. "I've answered enough of your questions. While Zhang is taking care of the cat-man, I should be doing my part." He took a step toward. "Any last words?"

"Do you have bones?"

"Of course," Quan said, and chuckled. "Why?"

"Just checking," Blade stated. Uncoiling his legs with the lightning speed of a striking panther, he swung both heels into the shapeshifter's left kneecap and heard a loud pop greet his effort.

Quan, amazingly, laughed. "That tickled," he remarked calmly, then tottered backward beyond the giant's reach. "You never give up, do you?"

Twisting and squirming, Blade tried to wriggle close enough to land another kick but the creature retreated even farther.

"You're wasting your time, Warrior," Quan told him. "Even if you broke every bone in my body, it wouldn't stop me." He bent down and touched his shattered knee, intense concentration lining his face.

Blade heard a groan on his left and discovered the Cavalryman had revived.

"Blade? What was the big idea walloping me?" Doc Madsen asked sluggishly. He licked his lips and gazed at the others. "And what's going on?"

"It wasn't me," Blade explained, nodding at the bogus Havoc. "We're up against a shapeshifter."

"A what?"

"An entity that can change its shape at will."

The gunfighter glanced at the motionless Havoc, his forehead creased, comprehension dawning. He tried his bonds, then looked down at his empty holster.

Blade had no time to explain everything. He rolled toward the creature, which promptly executed a sideways leap to carry it well out of danger.

Beaming, Zhongli Quan shook his injured leg. "The knee is nearly healed. My kind can repair any injury within minutes simply by focusing our minds on the wound. All you've done is caused me a little discomfort and temporary inconvenience."

"I'll try harder next time," Blade promised, continuing to roll, flexing his wrists as he did, striving to loosen the ropes enough to slip his hands out.

"There will be no next time," Quan stated. "I've tired of this game." So saying, he suddenly pounced, leaping onto the Warrior's chest and pinning the giant's shoulders down with his knees.

Blade promptly arched his spine, endeavoring to buck the creature off.

"No, you don't," Quan said, and slugged the Warrior on the jaw.

Despite Quan's smaller stature, Blade rocked with the blow, and would have passed out if not for the series of brutal slaps the creature then rained on his face. The intense stinging in his cheeks brought him around to see the thing sneering at him, its malevolent countenance seemingly floating in the air above him like a disembodied head.

"I've always wanted to beat someone to a pulp," Quan said, delivering a light tap to the giant's chin. "By the time I'm done, no one will be able to recognize you."

Blade's arms were pinned by the shapeshifter's knees and legs. To get it off his chest he resorted to an unconventional tactic. Whipping his hips upward, he made the shapeshifter lose its balance and tilt forward as he simultaneously drove his forehead into its face. The creature's nostrils crunched, blood spurted all over its face, and it scrambled off to the right, wiping its sleeve across its eyes.

The Warrior closed in and swung his body around, tucking his knees next to his chest. His sole hope, a feeble one at that, entailed keeping the thing off balance until he could get free. Unfortunately, the stout ropes resisted his every try.

Rising slowly, Quan appeared completely unconcerned, dabbing the last of the blood from his left eye. He didn't pay any attention to the giant.

Blade capitalized on the mistake by ramming his soles into the creature's legs and upending the monster, dropping it to the hard stone. He drew back his legs again.

"Enough!" Quan abruptly roared, and came off the ground in a burst of violent rage. He swatted the Warrior's legs aside and delivered a series of swift, fierce kicks to the giant's abdomen. "Enough of these games! Your days of meddling in the affairs of the Lords of Kismet are over."

Bunching into a ball to protect himself, Blade took the brunt of the kicks on his back and sides. The combat boots gouged into him, threatening to break a rib. One of the kicks whooshed the breath from his lungs and he went limp, his arms falling onto his thighs, exposed and vulnerable.

"And now we end this charade," Quan declared.

A black-clad figure rolled out of nowhere and hit the creature behind the legs, bowling it over. Doc Madsen pushed to his knees and clubbed it twice on the mouth, but he might as well have been striking armor plating.

Quan snarled and backhanded the gunman, flattening him. "Is there no end to your impertinence?" he demanded spitefully, rising. "In Asia humans know better than to lay a hand on their superiors."

Flooded with anguish, Blade braced his palms on the ground and crouched. He would continue to resist until his dying breath, if need be. His gaze fell on the pile of weapons, less than ten feet away.

"Don't even think of it," Quan said, and glided forward to seize the giant, wrenching him erect. His left hand clamped on the Warrior's throat. "I will tear out your heart and eat it raw."

A tremendous roar rent the air, echoing off the amphitheater wall and wafting out across the canyon, a roar that eloquently spoke of unbridled fury and excruciating misery commingled in a seething primal storm of long-suppressed emotions.

Quan pivoted, shock registering, and blurted, "Shiva preserve me!" He released the Warrior and stepped back.

Blade fell on his right side and twisted, suspecting the sight he would behold before he laid eyes on the source of the roar.

Fifteen feet away stood Grizzly, hunched over, his face the embodiment of elemental savagery, his fingers rigid, his five bearish claws fully extended. At his feet lay the severed ropes that had secured his arms and legs. His eyes blazed, stoked by inner fires of rampant bestiality. The creature called Quan stared at the bear-man's countenance, at those ten wicked claws, and did the unforeseen. He whirled and bolted.

Grizzly tore in pursuit.

"Wait!" Blade cried. "Cut us loose!" But his words were wasted on the hybrid, who chased the fleeing shape-shifter into the trees and was soon out of view. "Damn," he muttered, and got onto his hands and knees. Sliding his arms forward, he did the same with his knees and repeated the procedure until he reached the weapons. Eagerly he shoved M-16's aside and claimed both Bowies. It took but a moment to slice through the rope on his ankles, then to reverse his grip and finally free his hands.

"My turn, pardner."

Blade glanced around and saw Doc on his knees. Sparrow Hawk was awake, shaking his head and looking about in confusion. Lobo and Raphaela were both out. Blade rose and moved to the gunman's side.

"Why did that critter skedaddle?" Doc asked. "I figured it could hold its own against any of us."

"Strength-wise, maybe," Blade agreed, setting to work on the ropes. "But did you see its face when it laid eyes on Grizzly's claws? Maybe those things aren't as indestructible as they let on. Maybe it was afraid Grizzly would carve it into itty-bitty pieces."

"No, I didn't see the thing's face," Doc said. "I was too busy staring at Grizzly. What got into him? If you ask me, he went off the deep end."

Sparrow Hawk coughed. "Will someone kindly tell me what is happening?"

"Doc will," Blade said. "I'm going after Grizzly."

"And what should the rest of us do?" Doc asked.

The query gave Blade pause. In his anxiety over his old friend he was all too ready to leave his new people in the lurch. As much as he wanted to go to Grizzly's aid, he couldn't up and run off. "I've changed my mind. You distribute the weapons while I take care of the others."

"Now you're talking."

Blade hastened over to the Flathead.

"Are you going to knock me out again?" Sparrow asked, eyeing the giant warily.

"It wasn't me," Blade said, kneeling to cut the ropes, and went into a brief explanation.

"A shapeshifter?" Sparrow said when the Warrior finished. "My people had dealings with such creatures long before the whites came to these lands. I thought all of them were killed ages ago."

"Try to remember everything you can about them," Blade urged, stepping over to Raphaela to gently shake her shoulders. Immediately her eyes snapped wide and she recoiled, as if in fear of being struck. "It's me," Blade assured her. "You're safe now."

"What? Where's Grizzly?" Raphaela asked in confusion. She glanced toward Sparrow and cried, "He's the one who attacked me."

"Wrong," Blade said, moving to Lobo next, eager to get them all back on their feet and armed so they could go search for Grizzly and Jag. He was reaching for the Clansman's shoulder when a wailing scream pierced the canyon, the unmistakable cry of someone dying or on the verge of death. The wail lingered, became a gurgling whine, and expired.

CHAPTER FIFTEEN

"**D**id you really think you'd get away from me that easily?" the fake cat-man demanded, and snickered.

Halting abruptly, Jaguarundi crouched and curled his fingers, ready to employ his claws. He inhaled deeply, suppressing the pulsing pain in his body, and braced for the thing's onslaught.

Strangely, the shapeshifter made no move toward him. "You're tricky, catling. And you fight dirty."

"I'm just getting warmed up," Jag vowed.

"Sorry to disillusion you, but I've already won," the creature said.

"Could have fooled me."

"Only because you're ignorant of the full scope of our abilities. For instance, I'll bet you didn't know that we can transform in less than five seconds if need be," the shapeshifter said. "Here. Allow me to give you a demonstration."

Before Jag's astonished gaze the being suddenly altered its appearance again, the bones and skin shrinking, the body hair disappearing, blond locks sprouting on its head. In virtually no time at all the false hybrid was replaced by the little girl in the white dress. A sweet stench hovered in the air.

The child curtsied and said politely, "Hi. Remember me?"

Jag didn't bother answering. Here was a perfect opportunity to slay the thing before it changed into something more formidable, and he wasn't going to let the chance pass. He leaped forward, his right arm upraised.

Tittering, the child vaulted rearward ten feet and landed with all the grace and finesse of a practiced ballet dancer. "Naughty, naughty," she mocked him. "You're not nice."

Growling, Jag charged.

The shapeshifter laughed, gazed upward, and jumped over eight feet onto a tree branch, where it stood with its hands on its hips. "I have an idea. Why don't we play tag and you can be the one who is it?"

Jag stopped, glaring at the thing in frustration. How could he kill the taunting devil if he couldn't get close enough to use his nails?

"Since you're not very fond of human children, perhaps an adult will suffice," the shapeshifter said, and changed yet again, his facial features melting as if made of molten wax and instantly reforming even as the body grew and grew until it stood seven feet tall. A black vest solidified on its chest, fatigue pants on its legs. The new rugged countenance was all too familiar.

Uh-oh, Jag thought, moving backwards.

"Going somewhere?" asked the giant, dropping to the ground. He bunched his hands into fists, chuckled, and stepped slowly toward Jag. "And here I was under the impression that Blade and you are good friends."

The short hairs at the base of Jag's neck prickled. Observing the transformations was an unsettling, uncanny experience. The shapeshifter's bizarre ability seemed otherworldly, a feat defying every law of nature and logic. The uneasy feeling, combined with a peculiar revulsion at its calculated manipulations, inspired him with a flaming urge to rip the creature to shreds.

"Are you ready to die?" the shapeshifter asked.

"Are you?" Jaguarundi retorted, and attacked, springing at its chest with the intent of knocking it down.

The creature dodged to the left and aimed a terrific punch at the hybrid's temple.

Jag was ready, his feline physique every bit as quick as his namesake's. He evaded the punch and swiped his left hand across his adversary's abdomen, his inch-long nails tearing the black leather and digging into the flesh underneath. Blood dampened his fingertips, and then he was shifting to confront the shapeshifter head-on.

Incredulity lined the creature's face. Backing up, it pressed a hand to its ruptured abdomen and held blood-smeared fingers aloft. "You cut me, you bastard!"

"Stick around," Jag taunted. "I'll do more than that."

"Like hell you will!" the thing bellowed, initiating yet another change, becoming even larger and heavier, growing an extra set of arms in the bargain. All clothes vanished. Grayish, leathery skin now covered its nine-foot frame. The legs were squat, the arms long and slender, the hands capped with red fingernails. Sporting eyes the size of apples, an elongated face, and a crimson tongue that kept flicking out and in, the shapeshifter now resembled something out of a lunatic's nightmare.

Jag darted to the left and slashed at its thigh, but two of the creature's arms whipped out and grabbed his right wrist. He tried to jerk loose, but it pulled him toward its mouth, a gaping maw rimmed with tiny, pointed teeth that opened wide to chomp on him.

Kicking and flailing with his other arm, Jag vainly tried to gain his freedom.

"I'll eat you alive," the creature boasted.

"You talk too much," Jag said, and lunged, raking his left hand across the shapeshifter's face, slitting open its cheek. Automatically the creature brought its own hands upward to protect its eyes and moved rapidly backwards.

So it did have two weak spots! Jag realized, keeping the pressure on, concentrating on its groin and those oversized orbs. His claws dug furrows in the shapeshifter's arms as it endeavored to block him. In a frenzy he battered through its guard, and was about to rip its eyes from their sockets when the thing reversed direction and abruptly looped all four arms around him.

Jag's hands were pinned to his sides. He was suddenly lifted off the ground. Warm, fetid breath ruffled his facial fur as the thing bent its neck, about to bite his face in half. Two could play at that game, and despite the revulsion the act brought, Jag sank his teeth into the shapeshifter's chin.

Hissing, the creature reacted by jerking its head backwards, and in doing so tore a ragged gash in its flesh.

Jag found himself with a mouthful of shapeshifter and tasted tangy blood on his tongue. He spit the clump out and speared his mouth at the thing's neck, burying his teeth in the side of its neck.

In a frantic gesture the changeling gripped the hybrid's neck with two hands while shoving against the cat-man's chest with the other pair, desperately seeking to fling the feline from him.

Blood seeped down Jag's throat as he rocked his jaws back and forth, ripping a hole in the thing's neck. More blood sprayed onto his face, and with a start he discovered the shapeshifter's essential fluid was green, not red, and thinner than any blood had any right being, thinner than water even.

Roaring, the creature hurled the hybrid to the turf.

Jag came down on his shoulders and rolled to his feet, spitting bits of flesh and skin from his mouth. His animal nature struggled to supplant his human half, filling him with a craving to wade into the shapeshifter with his nails flying.

"You're more trouble than you're worth," the creature stated, placing its right palm over the gash on its chin. For a few moments it concentrated, and when the hand slipped aside the chin was whole once more. "Now do you understand why resistance is futile?"

"I understand that you're bluffing," Jag rasped, inching forward. "Sure, you can heal yourself, but how fast can you do it?"

"Fast enough."

"Let's find out," Jag said, and pounced.

They closed in a whirling flurry of multiple fists and ripping claws, each scoring repeatedly, each being cut or pounded in turn. Jag took a blow in the chest that nearly staved in his sternum. In retaliation he sliced the creature open from the left shoulder to the stomach. They fought and fought, always in motion, and both were spattered with the shapeshifter's blood when they finally separated and stood glaring at one another, catching their breaths for the next round.

"In all the years of my existence I've never been challenged like this," the creature said, winded and gasping, a score of green streaks crisscrossing his torso and limbs.

"There's more to come," Jag said.

"Only if you can catch me," replied the shapeshifter, who promptly wheeled and sped off.

Taken unawares, Jag took precious seconds to give chase. He didn't think he'd hurt the thing enough to justify its running off, and suspected there must be an ulterior motive, a trick intended to bring victory to the shapeshifter. Consequently he stayed farther back then he would have otherwise, ten feet behind as the creature plunged into shoulder-high grasses.

Abruptly, inexplicably, the thing vanished, shrinking out of sight in the blink of an eye.

Jag halted, scanning the vegetation, wondering where it had gone. He guessed that it had transformed again. Into what this time?

The grasses off to the left rustled and waved, as if something moved at their base.

A terrifying thought occurred to Jag. What if the things could change into animals, whether mammals, reptiles, amphibians, or whatever? So far the shapeshifter hadn't, but what was to stop it from becoming, say, a cobra or a rattlesnake? One bite and Jag would be done for. He rotated slowly, alert for his enemy.

Again the grasses rustled, farther to the left.

Coincidence? The cat-man doubted it. He backed up, wanting to get out of the grasses and in the clear where he could see the thing coming.

Something hissed, a sibilant, reptilian sound.

Positive he had guessed correctly, Jag focused on the ground, expecting the shapeshifter to slither out at him and try to sink its poisonous fangs into his feet or ankles. His head tilted downward, he nearly missed the next assault.

A short, thin form leaped out of the grasses in a flying arc, swooping toward the man-beast's head.

Out of the corner of his eye Jag detected the movement and instantly dropped into a crouch, looking up to behold an outlandish monstrosity sail over him.

The shapeshifter was now reptilian, all right, but unlike any reptile known in North America. Four feet long, as thick as a man's arm, it had dark green scales over its entire form, a head much like a snapping turtle's but with a pair of four-inch-long front fangs, and tiny *wings sprouting from the middle of its back.* Those wings flapped twice while the creature was airborne, and it flew into the grasses and disappeared.

Jag's skin crawled. What the hell had that thing been? He'd never seen anything like it. Had the shapeshifter assumed the form of a real creature perhaps existing in Asia, or was the winged horror a concoction of the shapeshifter's imagination?

The grasses on the right crackled.

Spinning, Jag took three bounds and leaped clear of the high grass into a narrow cleared space. He faced around, waiting for the flying miniature monster to show itself.

Instead, the shapeshifter transformed once more.

Jag heard heavy breathing and saw a large mass materialize, a brownish hulk that became bigger and bigger until in the span of seconds a hairy ape, a thing much like a gorilla but not a gorilla, stood erect, reaching ten feet in height. Its sloping forehead was pale, its eyes a striking hue of scarlet. The nostrils were much slimmer than any gorilla's that ever lived, and its lips were positively human in form.

The gorilla laughed, then spoke in a deep, booming voice. "Having fun, catling? I know I am."

"What are you now?" Jag inquired, stalling, his mind in high gear as he attempted to formulate a means of defeating the brute.

"A gorilla-man of Kunlun."

"There are no gorillas in Asia."

"There are now," the shapeshifter said, smirking. "The war was responsible. Asia and the western half of the Soviet Union received more fallout than all of the rest of the world combined. All sorts of new species have been mutated by the massive radioactivity."

"And that flying snake?"

"It's quite common in Sumatra."

"I thought maybe you made it up."

"We seldom do that, catling. It's difficult to create a new form from scratch," the creature said, moving toward the hybrid. "Mimicking beings or animals we know is easier and safer."

"And that thing with four arms?"

"Kali, cousin to Shiva, and one day destined to become a Lord of Kismet." The shapeshifter stalked clear of the high grass and crouched, its enormous muscles bulging. There was no evidence of the previous wounds inflicted by the hybrid.

Jag felt the creature was toying with him, enjoying the game of cat-and-mouse at his expense. He had to slay it and do so quickly. Sooner or later it would transform into something against which he would be helpless. Coiling his legs, he darted at the brute, extending his arms as if going for its bulbous gonads. In a reflexive action the shapeshifter lowered its arms to protect its privates, and at that instant Jag vaulted at its head, sinking his fingers and thumbs into the creature's eyes, rupturing both eyeballs.

The shapeshifter arched its back, venting a wailing scream.

In a blur Jag pressed his advantage, slicing into the thing's face and neck, mangling the throat and stripping the cheekbones bare of flesh. A fist caught him in the back and he dropped at its feet. The creature moaned and covered its head with its hands, evidently trying to repair the damage.

Not this time, bastard.

Jag speared his right hand into the gorilla-man's stomach, his sharp nails easily lancing through the abdominal wall. He gripped thick intestines and wrenched them out, then went to work in earnest, shredding the stomach, reducing the skin to tatters and severing every organ his fingers touched. A foul odor engulfed him, making him gag, and he retreated several yards.

The shapeshifter's wail lingered on. Its shoulders slumped and it feebly clasped its exposed abdominal cavity. Gurgling, blood spurting from its mouth, the creature tottered. "This can't be happening," it said in disbelief, then pitched onto its face with a pronounced thud. Shuddering and twitching, the shapeshifter blubbered a bit, then fell silent.

Jag waited, thinking that it might revert to whatever its natural form might be, but the creature stayed a gorilla. He kicked it once for good measure, turned, and headed toward the amphitheater. His job wasn't done. The Force was still in danger.

The second shapeshifter had to be dealt with.

CHAPTER SIXTEEN

"**H**ere comes the fur ball," Lobo announced.

Standing at the entrance to the amphitheater, in the act of slinging his M-16 over his left shoulder, Blade looked up and saw the cat-man racing toward them. All of the Force members had now been revived and were checking their weapons and comparing notes on the manner of their capture. They fell silent, gazing at the hybrid.

The Warrior noticed the greenish liquid and grisly gore spattered all over Jag's coat of fur and moved forward to greet him. "Are you okay?"

"Fine," Jag said, halting and scanning the others. "You guys?"

"We're in one piece."

"Where's Grizzly?"

"He took off after the shapeshifter named Quan," Blade disclosed. "What about the thing that chased you?"

Jag raised his right forefinger and slowly drew an imaginary line across the base of his throat.

"So they're not as indestructible as they like to pretend," Blade said thoughtfully.

"No, but they're damn hard to kill. If the one I fought

hadn't been playing with me, I wouldn't be here."

Raphaela walked up and placed a hand on Jag's shoulder. "I'm glad you're not hurt. We were worried about you."

Lobo snickered. "Speak for yourself, gorgeous."

"You were worried too," Raphaela said to the Clansman. "You're just too macho to admit it."

"You got the macho part straight," Lobo declared. "When they made me, they threw away the mold."

"Only because it was defective," Doc Madsen interjected.

Blade gazed at the rest. "Is everyone ready?"

They each nodded.

"Then let's get going. There's no time to lose," the Warrior advised, and looked at the hybrid. "Jag, lead the way but don't get out of our sight. The trail shouldn't be very hard to follow since neither of them were trying to conceal their tracks."

"Will do," the cat-man said, turning and scouring the ground. He found a set of Grizzly's footprints in soft soil and pointed. "Here we are."

"There's one thing you should know," Blade mentioned.

"What?" the beast-man replied.

"Grizzly went berserk. He might not have regained control yet."

Jaguarundi peered into the forest. "Thanks for the warning. When he loses it, he doesn't know what he's doing. No one is safe around him." Shaking his head, he moved off, his eyes glued to the ground.

"Move out, people," Blade commanded. "Single file. No more than five feet apart. And no talking." He paused. "That means you also, Lobo."

"Why are you always pickin' on me?"

"It must be your macho nature," Blade quipped,

jogging after the cat-man. The trail turned abruptly westward once they were in the trees, and in short order Blade deduced that the shapeshifter must have been making a beeline for the mouth of Dutchman Canyon.

As he ran, Blade pondered the possible significance of Zhongli Quan's actions. Fleeing from Grizzly made sense, if only because no one in their right mind, human or otherwise, wanted to be chopped into sushi by an enraged hybrid. But could there be another motive behind the shapeshifter's flight? And where would Quan go now that his presence in California had been uncovered?

A disturbing thought occurred to the Warrior. What if there were other shapeshifters in the Free State? If not, what if there were other clandestine operatives working for the Lords of Kismet? Since the Lords had assassins planted all over the globe, it was only natural that the Asian rules would have agents working for them in California too.

What if there existed an entire network of enemy operatives? From the information imparted by Quan, the Lords had another devilish scheme in the works. What was it this time? Given their track record, it must be something on a grand scale that would topple California, leaving the Freedom Federation weakened and ripe for conquest.

Another troubling aspect bothered him. Given the thoroughness with which the Lords formulated their plans, there must be contingencies worked out in advance in the event of mishaps. Quan probably could rely on others for assistance. Who were they? Where were they?

The Force pressed steadily westward, Jag slowing only once when he temporarily lost the prints on a rocky stretch. The closer they came to the canyon mouth, the faster they went. By two P.M. they were almost to the clearing where the convoy truck had dropped them off.

Jag slowed to allow his companions to overtake him.

"I don't believe it. From the deep impressions their feet made, Grizzly and that shapeshifter ran the whole way."

"Are we gaining on them?" Blade asked.

"I wish. They must be miles down the road by now."

Soon the Force reached the clearing and halted. Blade walked ahead, surveying the encircling tree line, and spied an odd, flattened cluster of vegetation located to the right of the road at the opposite end of the clearing. "What's that?" he asked, hurrying toward it, the rest right on his heels.

Lying on the grass was a makeshift camouflage latticework that would be eight feet high when upright and was 14 feet in length. It consisted of long, slender limbs tightly interwoven.

"What is this?" Raphaela asked.

Beyond the unusual affair was a wide cleared space in the woods. A pair of tire tracks led from the clearing, over the latticework, and onto the road.

"The shapeshifters hid two vehicles in there," Blade speculated. "Jeeps, most likely. Quan must have reached them first and taken off in one. Grizzly took the other."

"Then they're miles from here by now," Doc said.

"We'll never catch them," Sparrow added.

Raphaela stared down the narrow road. "Wait a minute. I'm not sure I understand. Those things hid the jeeps in the trees so we wouldn't see them?"

"Exactly," Blade confirmed. "They wanted us to believe we were stranded in Dutchman Canyon with no way out of the wilderness. If they'd left the jeeps in the open, any one of us who escaped their little trap could have gone for help."

"But why two jeeps? Why not just one?"

The Warrior shrugged. "Maybe they didn't want to be seen together after they killed us off. Maybe they had different places to go. I don't know."

"And what about Lieutenant Wharton? Was he working for them?"

"No, he was *one* of them, the same one who impersonated Gallagher," Blade guessed. "They wouldn't want any witnesses to their operation."

"But there was the guy who dropped us off," Lobo observed.

"Either he's in league with them or they planned to kill him once they finished with us," Blade said.

"Well, how are we going to get the hell out of here?" Lobo wondered. "We can't walk."

"Why can't we?" Blade responded.

"You're talkin' miles and miles. My tootsies can't take the strain."

"Your tootsies had better or we'll leave you behind," Blade proposed. About to resume their trek, he looked at the locked shack and was struck by an idea. "Doc, would you and Sparrow go break into that shack and tell me what's inside?"

"On our way, pardner," the gunfighter said.

"What do you think is in there?" Raphaela asked as the Cavalryman and the Flathead ran to do the giant's bidding.

"Maybe nothing we can use," Blade said. "But doesn't it strike you as odd that there isn't a phone out here?"

"In the middle of freakin' nowhere?" Lobo responded, and snorted.

"War exercises are held here regularly," Blade said patiently, as if explaining to a four-year-old. "The California Army prides itself on making mock combat sessions as realistic as possible. Under such grueling conditions, occasionally a soldier must be injured."

"Yeah? So?" Lobo said.

"So how would the officer in charge contact medical

personnel or request an airborne evacuation in an emergency?''

Lobo watched Sparrow Hawk and Doc Madsen batter their shoulders against the wooden door. "Send a vehicle back. How else?"

"We'll soon know."

On the sixth try the wooden panel cracked. A seventh splintered the wood and Doc went inside, emerging seconds later to sprint back with a grin on his face. "How did you know?" he asked.

"What did you find?" Blade inquired.

"Blankets, rations, medical supplies, and a portable field phone."

"Bingo," Blade said, hurrying toward the shack. "We'll be out of here in no time."

Lobo held back as the others followed the giant. He grasped Raphaela's fatigue shirt and said softly, "Hold up a sec."

"What's the matter?" she asked him.

"Do you think Blade is a mutant?"

Raphaela started to laugh, saw he was serious, and uttered a most unladylike chortle. "Where *do* you get your crazy ideas?"

"What's so crazy about this one?" Lobo rejoined.

"Blade is as human as you or I," Raphaela stated.

"Well, me anyway."

"You're turnin' into a real smartass, sister."

"I'm sorry. But the idea is ridiculous."

"Is it? Haven't you noticed the way he always figures things out that nobody else can? It's spooky."

"He uses his brain. It wouldn't hurt if you tried doing the same."

"Very funny. I'm tellin' you that Blade ain't fully human. I bet his mother was a hybrid."

"Do you want me to ask him?"

Lobo recoiled in shock. "Are you wacko? He'd tie me into knots if he found out I was pryin' into his personal life. Just forget I ever brought the subject up."

"Gladly," Raphaela said, grinning and started to go.

"And remember that I was the one who warned you when the truth finally comes out."

"You're really something. Do you know that?"

"Sure do. Every fox tells me the same thing. That's what I get for being a Grade-A hunk."

Raphaela laughed all the way to the shack.

Two hours later a pair of jeeps finally arrived at the clearing. The lead vehicle braked near the shack, where the Force sat waiting, and the sergeant doing the driving threw the gearshift into park, hopped out, and saluted the giant who walked up to him.

"Sergeant Dresden at your service, sir."

"It took you long enough," the Warrior remarked.

"Sorry, sir, but we had to drive all the way from L.A.," Dresden noted. "We did the best we could."

"Did you happen to pass any other jeeps on your way here?"

"No, sir, I don't believe we did."

"Then get us to the Force Facility pronto," Blade instructed, taking a seat on the passenger side.

The other Force members divided up and climbed into the vehicles. Raphaela and Lobo joined the Warrior, getting in the back.

"How will we find General Gallagher and Grizzly now?" the Molewoman asked.

"I don't know," Blade confessed.

Sergeant Dresden, sliding behind the wheel, glanced at the giant. "Excuse me, sir, I couldn't help but overhear."

"Yes?"

"I might be able to help you locate General Gallagher."

Blade swung toward the noncom. "How?"

"Whenever vehicles are taken from the motor pool, they must be signed for. Whoever does the taking has to specify a destination and a return time."

"That's standard procedure, I understand. So?"

"So the general signed two jeeps out of the motor pool at Headquarters in L.A. yesterday morning. One is supposed to be returned tonight by a Sergeant Havoc. The other is being dropped off at the motor pool at Oakland Army Base."

"Near San Francisco?"

"Yes, sir. Right across the bay."

Blade startled the noncom by reaching out and tweaking the man's right cheek. "Sergeant, you're wonderful."

"I am?" Dresden replied dubiously.

"Yes," Blade said, nodding. "Take us to Oakland Army Base and don't worry about the speed limit."

"But my captain is expecting us to return to Los Angeles."

"I'll call him from Oakland and explain the situation," Blade said, his voice hardening. "This is a direct order, Sergeant."

"Yes, sir," Dresden said, shifting into drive. "You're the boss. General Gallagher gave us orders ages ago to do whatever you want, anytime you want."

The irony made Blade grin. "How nice of the general."

"May I ask why you're in such a hurry to find him?"

"Certainly," Blade said, tucking the M-16 between his legs. "I plan to blow his brains out."

CHAPTER SEVENTEEN

Zhongli Quan was furious.

In the guise of General Miles Gallagher he raced northwestward on Interstate 5, heading for Oakland, the wind brushing his bulldog face, the brilliant afternoon sun making him squint against the glare on the jeep's windshield. Since Zhang had signed the vehicle out at the motor pool in L.A. while in the form of the general, Zhongli had to drop it off as the same person. Originally, their plan had called for Zhang to make the trip to San Francisco area and for him, as Sergeant Havoc, to take the second jeep back to Los Angeles.

Now everything was all screwed up.

Zhongli knew his fellow Gualaon had perished. He'd felt Zhang's death shriek in his mind. Gualaons shared an intense mental rapport; when in close proximity to one another they could actually "feel" each other's presence, although, regretfully, they were incapable of telepathic communication such as the Chimereans enjoyed. But then the Chimereans relied more on their minds anyway.

He gazed into the rearview mirror and saw the hybrid's jeep almost a mile behind. Good. Let the fool keep coming.

Once he arrived in Oakland, a quick phone call to the San Francisco Assassin Cell would result in a suitable reception for the genetic deviate. He couldn't wait to spring the trap.

A sign on the right indicated the junction with 580 was not far ahead.

The shapeshifter idly watched the essentially flat countryside streak past. Memories of his cherished Mongolia prompted him to yearn for his rugged homeland, for the starkly picturesque plateaus and towering mountain ranges that covered much of the country. Then there was the Gobi Desert, where he'd spent much of his later childhood, where the dry, blistering winds and the constantly shifting sands had made the very earth seem alive.

He hoped the Lords of Kismet would permit him to return home after his current assignment was successfully concluded. The longer he stayed in the Free State of California, the less he liked it. Humankind's so-called civilizations were tremendously distressing to one who favored remote wilderness. California reminded him all too vividly of the prewar culture in America, of the crass selfishness and materialism that had been rampant, of the sordid rape of the planet done in the dubious name of industry and commerce.

Give him the plateaus, the steppes, and the mountains any day.

It was distressingly typical of humans to pollute everything they touched. He'd often compared them to cockroaches, only he believed cockroaches were cleaner in their habits. Humans scurried about without rhyme or reason, breeding like rats, bipedal vermin who deserved to be completely exterminated. It was too bad they'd botched the job with World War Three.

Zhongli longed for the future day when the crafty Lords of Kismet finally achieved their goal of total domination of the human species. Once all humans were reduced to the deserved status of slaves, the Lords and their allies, the Gualaons, Chimereans, and others, could get on with the business of making the world a truly better place in which to live.

Hopefully, it wouldn't take more than a few hundred years.

He shook his head, dispelling his train of thought, concentrating on the here and now and the problems presented by the failure of the plan to eliminate the Force and place the blame on Jaguarundi. If he'd been smart he would have prevailed on Zhang to slay the Force members the moment they were captured instead of waiting to kill them all at once. But Zhang had insisted on being his usual methodical self, on having all of the scum in the palm of his hand before eradicating them. And look at what had happened!

If only he'd known about the bear-man's claws! Zhongli shivered at the recollection of seeing them, thinking of the damage they could do to a Gualaon, to him. Of the few ways to slay his kind, the most effective consisted of chopping Gualaons into small parts and rendering their healing ability completely useless. Back in ancient times, when most humans had carried swords of one kind or another, Gualaons had been extra cautious in their dealings with mortals.

He was annoyed at himself for panicking. But the supremely fierce expression the bear-man had worn left no doubt that the hybrid would have torn into him with a frenzy unequaled in his vast experience.

Maybe he was simply turning cowardly in his old age. After so many centuries he'd grown rather fond of living and felt no inclination to end his existence soon. Of course, he couldn't let the Lords know the details of his flight from a mere hybrid; they would be most displeased, and

VENGEANCE STRIKE 163

displeasing them was the same as committing suicide.

In five minutes Zhongli reached 580, and bore westward until he hit the former Interstate Highway 880, now simply referred to as the Nimitz Freeway since the interstate system no longer officially existed. Turning to the north, he passed the Oakland Airport and the Coliseum. The traffic became terribly congested. He stayed in the passing lane, traveling just above the speed limit, periodically verifying the hybrid was still on his tail.

Keep coming, fool.

You'll get yours soon.

He didn't need to bother with presenting identification when he arrived at the Oakland Army Base gate. Both guards snapped to attention at the sight of his uniform and familiar countenance, which hung on display at every installation in the State along with photographs of the governor and other top military leaders. Every soldier in the California Army knew of General Gallagher and his reputation as a hardass. In his own way, the real Gallagher had been almost as famous as Blade.

Thinking of the Warrior brought a frown. Of all the humans in North America, perhaps even on the globe, the giant from Minnesota posed the greatest threat to the Lords of Kismet. Ironically, the Warrior didn't even know it.

Zhongli dropped off the jeep at the motor pool, used the phone there to place his call to Fangio, borrowed ten bucks from a sergeant, then hurried to the gate and grabbed a cab for the trip across the bridge into the City by the Golden Gate.

Predictably, the hybrid followed.

The shapeshifter grinned wickedly in anticipation.

During the course of the long drive from Dutchman Canyon to Oakland Grizzly's raging fury had gradually subsided and he'd regained control of his surging emotions. He'd been compelled to sheath his claws upon reaching the jeep in order to drive, and doing so had helped dramatically to cool his boiling blood, serving, as it often did, as a pyschological trigger that brought his human self to the forefront and sublimated his bestial nature for the time being.

Initially he'd tried his damnedest to overtake the shapeshifter, but his jeep wasn't built for speed and he'd resigned himself to simply shadowing the creature to its destination. He'd dropped back about a mile, staying behind other vehicles much of the way, hoping thereby to give the shapeshifter the illusion of being in the clear. At the base he'd pulled into a parking lot across the street and waited for the phony officer to reappear, knowing it would be foolish to confront the creature on the base because other soldiers would undoubtedly rush to the defense of their presumed superior and he had no desire to slay innocents.

The shapeshifters were responsible for breaking up Athena and him.

The shapeshifters would pay the price.

Grizzly felt guilty about deserting his friends in Dutchman Canyon, but not guilty enough to turn around and go back. Blade and company could handle themselves. The other creature might already be dead, which bothered the bear-man a little. He wanted to take them both out, but he'd settle for this one.

Now he stiffened as he saw the general hail a taxi just outside the gate. Shifting, he waited until the cab went over a block before pulling out into the traffic flow and trailing it. He hadn't expected the shapeshifter to leave so soon after arriving, but he wasn't about to look the proverbial gift horse in the mouth. He'd see where it went, then rip the son of a bitch to shreds.

Many were the curious and appalled stares directed his way by quite a few drivers and pedestrians. He ignored them all. Some, he figured, would deduce his identity from the photographs of him published in various California newspapers. Just so no well-intentioned do-gooder reported him to the authorities and a black-and-white sporting flashing lights showed up to investigate. The commotion would alert the creature.

The car drove across the San Francisco-Oakland Bay Bridge and wound up on Bryant Street. After going several blocks it took a left, entering a warehouse district. In a minute the taxi braked in front of a huge gray structure bordering a series of train tracks. Out hopped the creature, who paid off the cabbie and hurriedly entered the warehouse through a pair of double doors.

Grizzly had pulled over to the curb when the taxi stopped. He observed it leave, impatiently let two minutes elapse, then got out of the jeep and padded toward the side of the building. A few passersby gawked at him and he ignored them.

A wide alley flanked the west side of the warehouse. He went along the base of the wall, peering up at the large windows 15 feet overhead, until he came to the rear. A glance revealed a lot crammed with piles of wood, black metal barrels, rolls of wire, and other materials. A lone door was situated at the center of the wall.

Grizzly stealthily advanced and cautiously took the knob in his right hand. A slight twist confirmed it wasn't locked. He slowly eased the door outward, his keen ears straining to pinpoint his enemy. Only silence greeted his attempt.

He peered inside to find the warehouse contained mountains of building supplies. What would the shapeshifter be doing here? he wondered, puzzled. Slipping in took but a second, and he sought shelter behind a stack of two-by-fours. The interior was much cooler than outside, the concrete floor smooth under the soles of his feet. A musty scent hung in the air.

Grizzly surveyed the piles, stacks, and mounds of assorted materials. Nothing moved. Perhaps there was an office somewhere in the building. His best bet to find the bogus general would be there.

Exhibiting consummate stealth, a shadow among shadows, Grizzly launched a search for his quarry. He went up one aisle and down another. Nowhere did he find an office, nowhere the shapeshifter. When he halted beside a pallet bearing scores of bags of cement a strange feeling came over him, an inexplicable conviction that he wasn't alone, a certainty that the hunter had become the hunted.

In confirmation a mocking voice called out from off to the right, "How nice of you to make our job so much easier."

Grizzly crouched, recognizing General Miles Gallagher's gruff tone. Which meant the creature was still impersonating the officer.

"You can answer us," the shapeshifter baited him. "We know where you are."

We? Grizzly glanced right and left. Why did the creature keep using the plural? Who else was in the warehouse?

"My friends and I are looking forward to some entertainment," the thing declared. "I hope you won't disappoint us."

Spinning, Grizzly ran to the next junction and took a left. He paused, expecting to hear the sound of pursuit.

"There's no sense in trying to escape us," said the shapeshifter. "We have eyes everywhere."

What kind of eyes? Grizzly asked himself, and discovered the answer the very next instant when he bent his neck to gaze far overhead at the sturdy beams crisscrossing the underside of the roof. There, firmly anchored to a steel beam, was a video camera. A tiny blinking red light on the outer facing indicated the unit was in use.

Grizzly sprinted deeper into the bowels of the building. He wasn't about to call it quits because the opposition had pulled a fast one on him. They would learn the hard way that tricking him and taking him down were two different things.

"Where do you think you're going?" the shapeshifter yelled. "Why delay the inevitable? We have you surrounded."

On top of a mountain of crates directly ahead materialized a skinny man attired all in black, including a black hood. In his left hand he held a gleaming Oriental sword. He stared brazenly at the hybrid for a bit, then swung around, walked to the end of the stack, and simply jumped from sight.

Grizzly poured on the speed, eager to catch one of them. But when he came to the opposite side of the crates there was no man in black in sight. He walked down the aisle, stooped at the waist and ready for the assault to come. Or so he believed. He heard the whispering of feet across the floor behind him and spun. There was no one there.

These guys are good, Grizzly thought, doing an about-face, and bristled at spying *another* person in black not 20 feet off. Instead of a katana, this one had a six-foot-long bamboo blowgun pressed to his lips.

The man exhaled loudly.

A small red dart shot out and streaked toward the hybrid. Grizzly tried throwing himself to the left to avoid it, but the point hit him in the right shoulder and stuck fast, imbedded at least an inch, causing an intense stinging pain.

Irritated more than hurt, Grizzly yanked the nuisance out and took several strides toward the figure, who stupidly made no attempt to flee. Talk about idiots! He began to extend his fingers, about to pop his claws out, when a burning sensation flared in his shoulder and spread rapidly down his arm and into his chest. His heart pounded for several beats, then seemed to freeze up. His whole body went rapidly numb. Stunned, he tried to keep moving, but his legs refused to cooperate. His last conscious act was to glance down at the dart tip and note the bluish substance coating the lower third of the needle.

I've been poisoned! Grizzly thought, and toppled onto his face.

CHAPTER EIGHTEEN

Grizzly heard a loud groan and realized he was making the sound. He tried to collect his thoughts, but they flitted about in his mind like elusive hummingbirds. His shoulders ached terribly and his body felt as if he'd been caught in an avalanche and battered mercilessly. Easing his eyes open, he took stock of his situation.

He seemed to be floating in a wispy haze that obscured everything in his immediate vicinity. His feet dangled off the floor. For a few moments he wasn't certain whether he was dreaming or awake.

And then *she* appeared, dressed in fatigues.

Grizzly recoiled in bewilderment when she strolled casually toward him out of the mist, a veritable angel if ever there was one, a welcoming smile creasing her lovely features, her fine brown hair swaying as she walked. "It can't be!" he blurted out.

She halted in surprise. "What's the matter, lover? Don't you know who I am?"

"You're dead," Grizzly declared. "I saw Death Master kill you with my own eyes."

"You only think you did."

He blinked, uncetain, his perception of reality askew. Was it possible? Had he imagined her death? No, it had been all too vivid, too ghastly. "Like hell, Athena," he stated harshly. "This can't be happening."

Athena Morris walked slowly, seductively over to him and tenderly reached up to caress his chin. "What's gotten into you? Has Blade's brainwashing taken effect?"

"Blade?" Grizzly repeated in confusion. "What are you talking about?"

"Don't you remember? Blade has been trying to destroy the Force for months."

"You've got it all wrong. General Gallagher is the one who has tried to ruin us."

"No, lover," Athena said, running her fingers over his hairy chest. "I'm afraid that you're the one who has it backwards. Gallagher has been working *with* us, trying to help us thwart the Warrior's scheme. If you weren't brainwashed, you'd know all this."

Grizzly was utterly confounded. His swirling mind prevented him from concentrating long enough to formulate a logical rebuttal. He knew she couldn't possibly be right, and yet he found himself tending to believe her testimony over his own vague recollections. "This can't be happening."

"Why can't it?" Athena asked, stroking his arm.

"Because Blade would never turn on us. He's the best friend any of us have ever had."

Athena clucked and patted his arm. "You poor baby. What has he done to you?"

Feeling suddenly nauseous, Grizzly blinked and licked his extremely dry lips. He tried to sort fact from fiction and a searing headache abruptly developed.

"How can you doubt me?" Athena asked.

Her words echoed hollowly in Grizzly's cranium and he sagged. What was wrong with him? What had happened? Why couldn't he remember? His sentience faded, and the last sound he heard before he slipped under was Athena's whispered sentence.

"Give him another dose."

He came around slowly, every fiber of his being weighted with oppressive sluggishness. When he opened his eyes he found the mist much worse, a fog that completely engulfed him. He hurt like hell.

Out of the fog came Athena Morris, smiling, to halt in front of him. "I'm here to save you," she said.

"Where am I?" Grizzly asked, experiencing difficulty in moving his mouth.

"Blade captured you. You're in a warehouse in San Francisco."

Grizzly's brow furrowed as he attempted to remember. "Blade wouldn't hurt me. You must be mistaken."

A sigh fluttered from her deliciously red lips. "I'm disappointed in you, lover. How long will this take?"

"Will what take?"

"You're being stubborn, lover," Athena said, and looked past him. "Give him another dose."

"Dose?" Grizzly repeated. "Dose of what?" A sharp pricking sensation in his lower back made him wince, and before he knew it the fog faded to black.

Dimly he knew someone was stroking his abdomen. Faintly he heard a soft, crooning voice.

"—to help you, honey. I'll save you. Blade is trying to use you to destroy the Force. We can't let that happen."

Grizzly's eyes fluttered wide and he discovered he was suspended in the center of gray pea soup. Athena Morris stood beside him, gazing expectantly into his face.

"At last! I thought he'd killed you."

"Who?"

"Blade. The Warrior knocked you out and brought you to a warehouse to finish you off."

"Why would Blade do such a thing? He's our leader."

"He's not the read Blade."

"What?"

"Blade was killed several weeks ago by a shapeshifter who took his place on the squad. Don't you remember?"

"No," Grizzly confessed, his mind a blank state. He gazed at her and felt uneasy.

"What's wrong?"

"I don't know. I have this odd feeling that you shouldn't be here."

Athena moved back a step. "You're impossible, lover. No one has ever resisted this long before."

"I don't understand."

She frowned and said, "Give him another dose."

From behind the man-beast came a response.

"Three could kill him."

"I don't give a damn. Administer another dosage immediately."

Grizzly tried to twist his head to glimpse the speaker, but couldn't. Something lanced into his left shoulder and vertigo swept him into oblivion.

"Grizzly?"

He heard her voice and his heart rejoiced. Gladly he snapped awake and saw his beloved standing there a yard away. A mist partially shrouded both of them. "Athena!"

"How are you?" she inquired in concern, moving closer.

Grizzly felt lethargic but otherwise okay. He seemed to be hanging in midair, his feet not quite touching the floor. Baffled as to the reason, he attempted to recall the circumstances preceding his awakening and could not. In fact, he couldn't remember a thing other than the fact he loved Athena Morris and was indescribably overjoyed at seeing her again. "Fine, I think. Where am I? How did I get here?"

"The phony Blade knocked you out and brought you to this abandoned warehouse."

"What do you mean by phony?"

"A shapeshifter has assumed the Warrior's identity. It's trying to destroy the Force from within."

"I've never heard of such a creature. Where is this shapeshifter now?"

Athena radiated a broad smile. "He'll be here soon, I would imagine. If I set you free, will you help me kill him?"

"What kind of a stupid question is that? Sure I will."

"You're positive?"

Grizzly impatiently motioned with his arms and heard the rattling of chains. "Are you sure *you're* all right? If some kind of creature has infiltrated the squad, it's up to us to deal with it."

"I'm so happy to hear you say that," Athena said, producing a key from her pants pocket. She stepped into the mist, and returned carrying a short stepladder that she placed alongside him and climbed. "I'll have you down in a jiffy."

Grizzly gazed at the mist, striving his utmost to remember what had happened to him. His memory seemed to have been totally erased. How could such a thing happen? A troubling thought struck him and he glanced at Athena. "Hey, if this creature has taken Blade's identity, where's the Warrior?"

Her eyes mirroring an acute sadness, Athena answered quietly, "He's dead. The thing killed him."

A low growl rumbled in Grizzly's chest. Blade had been one of his best friends. He'd see that the sucker responsible paid in spades. "Where's the rest of the Force?"

"They're with the shapeshifter. None of them know about the switch. They mistakenly believe he's the real Blade."

"We'll have to set them straight."

"It won't be easy," Athena commented, her arms stretched above his head. "He's convinced them that you've gone renegade. They won't accept a word you say."

"Then I'll take the damn thing down without their help," Grizzly vowed.

"You'll have me to back you up."

"What more could a guy ask for?" Grizzly quipped, and unexpectedly dropped to the floor as the pressure around his wrists subsided. He craned his neck and saw shackles swinging overhead. They were attached to heavy chains suspended from the ceiling. "Thanks, gorgeous."

"Any time, lover," Athena said, climbing down the stepladder. She stepped up and gave him a swift kiss on the cheek. "We'd better find a spot to hide until the Force arrives. If we give ourselves away, the fake Blade might take off before we have him right where we want him."

Grizzly lifted his hands. "I want the son of a bitch on the business end of my claws."

"Then let's go."

The bear-man followed Athena, walking only a few yards before they emerged from the unusual cloud. He sniffed the air and grabbed her arm.

"What's wrong?"

"Men are here. I can smell them."

"They were here," Athena corrected him. "Three of Blade's henchmen were driving off just as I arrived."

"How did you find me?"

"I overheard the shapeshifter talking on the phone back at the Facility."

"Where is this warehouse located, by the way?"

"In San Francisco."

Grizzly stared at a high pile of lumber on their right. "There are plenty of hiding places. The shapeshifter won't stand a chance. I'll rip the bastard to pieces before he knows what hit him."

Athena looked over her shoulder and grinned. "I was hoping you'd say that."

Night had descended by the time the Force arrived at Oakland Army Base. Blade presented his I.D. to the gate guards, who promptly fell all over themselves in an effort to be of the utmost assistance, and learned from one of them that General Miles Gallagher had arrived hours ago, left a jeep at the motor pool, and taken a taxi. The officer was last seen heading over the San Francisco-Oakland Bay Bridge.

"Did you happen to see any sign of another member of the Force, a hybrid resembling a bear?" Blade inquired.

"No, sir," one of the men replied.

The Warrior turned and discovered a row of cabs waiting along the curb. Apparently the taxis did a brisk business shuttling servicemen to and from the base and staked it out daily. He looked at Sergeant Dresden. "Will you wait here for me?"

"Whatever you want, sir, you get."

Blade walked over to where a group of cab drivers were clustered in conversation. "Excuse me," he interrupted them.

The six men faced him wearing varying expressions of amazement.

"Aren't you that Blade guy?" a portly cabbie asked.

"Yeah, the one we read about in the papers all the time?" chimed in another.

"I am," Blade confirmed. "And I need your help."

"We'll be glad to help out the head honcho of the

Force," said a lean driver.

"Good. Did any of you happen to take General Miles Gallagher into San Francisco earlier today?"

The portly man shrugged. "We take a lot of officers all over. What does this Gallagher look like?"

"Sort of like a bulldog in a bad mood."

The lean driver brightened. "Yeah, I remember him. Real grumpy puss. Had me take him to the warehouse district."

Blade became tense in expectation. "Can you remember the address?"

"Not offhand."

The giant frowned.

"But I've got it written down in my fare book. Give me a minute and I'll look it up," the cabbie offered.

"Please," Blade said eagerly, and walked with the man to his yellow cab.

"Is this guy a friend of yours?" the driver inquired as he slid in behind the wheel.

"We're old acquaintances. Why do you ask?"

"Because of the funny look you had on your face."

"It's just that I'm excited about seeing him again. I hope he's still there."

"A surprise, is it?"

Blade nodded somberly. "I hope it's the biggest surprise of his life."

CHAPTER NINETEEN

"**D**rive past the warehouse," Blade instructed as they approached the address the cabbie and supplied. "I want to study the layout."

"Yes, sir," Sergeant Dresden replied.

They were still a few hundred feet from the building when their headlights revealed a military jeep parked at the curb. Dresden slowed.

"That must be the one Grizzly drove," Raphaela guessed.

The giant nodded and motioned for them to proceed. They continued past the enormous structure and around the block. "Park behind that jeep," he directed.

The noncom immediately obeyed.

Blade hopped out and motioned for his people to gather around. He glanced at Dresden and said, "Stay here until we return. If we're not back in twenty minutes, go for help."

The noncom gazed at the closed double doors, thinking of the information the Warrior had imparted on the trip into the metro area. "Do you think that thing is still in there?"

"I hope so," Blade stated. "If we don't nail it now, there's no telling where it will show up again or whose identity it will take."

Jaguarundi was staring apprehensively at the other jeep. "What could have happened to Grizzly?"

"We'll soon know," Blade said, sweeping all of them with an intent gaze. "You're all aware of what we're up against. Since the thing can assume any shape it wants, it can easily impersonate any of us. To prevent it from doing so, once we're inside don't let those you are with out of your sight."

"Maybe one of us should stay here with Dresden and help guard the jeeps," Lobo suggested. "I'll be glad to do it."

"You're coming with the rest of us."

"Okay, but don't blame me if that freak steals our wheels and gets away."

Blade turned and headed for the warehouse, surveying the darkened windows for signs of movement. His gut instinct told him they were walking into a trap. Unfortunately, they had no alternative. The shapeshifter must be destroyed at all costs. And they would have to do the job themselves; calling in Regular Army troops for assistance would only compound the problem because Quan would probably flee if the odds were too overwhelming.

He suppressed his mounting anxiety over Grizzly. There had been plenty of time for the hybrid to catch up with Quan and slay him. What if the shapeshifter had prevailed? He braced himself emotionally in case they should find Grizzly's body inside.

The Warrior halted when only ten feet from the entrance and addressed his unit. "Here's the way we're going to do this. Doc, you'll take Lobo and Sparrow Hawk and go around back. There must be a rear door. We'll wait here for exactly one minute, then go in. Synchronize your watch with mine so you enter at the same time."

The Cavalryman pulled back the sleeves on his left wrist, exposing the same kind of watch issued to all of them upon their arrival in the Free State. "I have twenty minutes past nine."

"I have eighteen past," Blade said, "which really doesn't matter. When your second hand hits the half-past mark, take off. I'll count down sixty seconds on my watch."

Jaguarundi, eyeing the warehouse, remarked, "I just hope Grizzly is all right."

"You don't need to worry about Fuzz Face," Lobo said. "He can lick twenty guys with one arm tied behind his back."

"But we're not up against humans," Jag noted.

Blade, watching Doc's second hand reach the 30 mark, nodded at the gunfighter. "Take off."

Slinging his M-16 over his left shoulder, Madsen spun and ran around the corner with Lobo and Sparrow in tow, the Flathead hefting his spear.

"I have a bad feeling about this," Jag said when they were gone.

"Do you think something has happened to Grizzly?" Raphaela asked.

"It's not that so much as I sense—something," Jag said, and gestured at the doors. "Something is in there. I know it."

"Probably the shapeshifter," Raphaela said.

Engrossed in keeping track of the ticking seconds, Blade glanced up at a window high above them and glimpsed a vague shape standing there. But at the very instant he laid eyes on it, the figure retreated from view.

"Did you see that?" Jag asked.

The Warrior nodded, focusing on the timepiece. When

the 60 seconds went by, he pivoted and stalked to the double doors, the M-16 in his left hand. He twisted the right-hand knob, and wasn't the least bit surprised to discover the door unlocked. Yanking it open, he slid inside and to the right, crouching with his back to the wall, his finger curling around the trigger.

Jag and Raphaela emulated his example, the cat-man moving to the left, Raphaela simply advancing a yard and halting.

Without warning the overhead lights flared on throughout the warehouse, illuminating scores of pallets piled high with various construction supplies.

The hybrid sniffed the air and announced, "Grizzly is here somewhere. His scent is strong." He paused, sniffing again. "There are others here too. Humans, from their odor. Must be several."

"And the shapeshifter?" Blade queried softly.

"Hard to tell. Those things can smell like anything."

"Stay close," Blade said, and advanced down a wide aisle between the stacked items. He peered toward the rear, but couldn't see Doc and the rest because the aisle they were using, like many others, didn't extend in a straight line; it curved or cut abruptly one way or another.

"Footsteps," Jag said. "Off to the left."

"I don't hear anything," Raphaela whispered.

"There's someone there," Jag stated. "Trust me."

Blade saw a shadow flit between two pallets on the left side. He trained the M-16 in that direction, anticipating an attack. Suddenly, from the back of the warehouse, an M-16 chattered.

At the same moment a furry form hurtled from the top of stacked crates on their right, diving straight at the Warrior.

"It's time," Doc Madsen had informed Sparrow and

Lobo almost a minute earlier. He tried the rear door, which opened readily enough, and glided within, his right hand hovering next to his Magnum.

The Flathead came in and squatted, listening. As with the gunfighter, he had his rifle slung over a shoulder. He much preferred to employ the weapons he was accustomed to using in close combat, and he held the spear at waist height, his stocky body coiled for action.

Lobo entered brazenly, making no attempt to keep low, his M-16 leveled, his cocky bearing an extension of his smug attitude. "Let's get this over with. I want to get back to the barracks and crash. Where is this thing?"

Doc thought about warning the Clansman not to be so overconfident. Lobo, after all, had been unconscious when Blade fought Quan. The Clansman didn't truly appreciate the creature's ferocity.

The lights abruptly came on.

"They know we're here," Lobo said.

Sparrow moved forward a few yards, then paused. "Someone is watching us."

"Who? Where are they?" Lobo inquired, glancing in all directions. "I don't see anyone."

"I don't either. I just know we are being watched."

"Don't start with that Indian mumbo jumbo," Lobo said.

"I know what I know."

"Yeah, right. I think you've been livin' in the woods too long, if you get my drift."

"Quiet, both of you," Doc stated, stepping ahead of them and surveying the stacked supplies on both sides of the aisle. Out of the corner of his eye he detected motion, and swung toward a pallet containing sacks of cement mix.

On top of the sacks, a crossbow pressed to his shoulder, was a man dressed all in black. A black hood covered his face. On the forehead of the hood was a bright red design or insignia.

Doc took in the details in the blink of an eye, then hurled himself aside even as the bowman released a short shaft that sped across the intervening distance and narrowly missed his chest. The arrow went through the flap of his frock coat, struck the concrete floor, and ricocheted off, zinging into a tidy pile of lumber and thudding into a board.

"Look out!" Lobo cried, too late, while snapping off a burst.

The man in the hood spun and darted from sight a millisecond before powerful slugs ripped into the sacks.

"Damn! I missed," Lobo grumbled.

Standing beside dozens of metal drums piled four high and six deep, Doc scanned the top of the opposite row of supplies, expecting the next attack to also come from the heights. Nor was he wrong. A black-shrouded head materialized at the edge of a high row of crates and a blowgun jutted out, aimed at the Clansman. This new assassin hadn't yet spied Doc.

In a smooth flow of movement the gunfighter drew his Smith and Wesson, thumbing back the hammer as the big revolver leaped clear of the holster. He fired without consciously aiming, simply by bending his elbow, pointing the barrel at the red marking on the killer's hood, and squeezing off a single shot.

The man stiffened, clutched at his forehead, and collapsed.

Doc took a step, seeking more attackers, his eyes on the opposite row of supplies. He realized the gravity of his mistake when Lobo screamed again.

"Behind you!"

Pivoting, Doc found another man in black, this one bearing a long, slightly curved sword, racing around the end of the drums. In three bounds the swordsman reached the gunman's side and lifted the sword overhead for a killing stroke. Doc extended the Magnum and started to fire.

Instead of going for the head or chest, the swordsman swept the glittering weapon down at the gunfighter's gun arm.

Blade was unable to bring the M-16 to bear before the figure slammed into him, knocking him flat and sending the rifle flying. He looked up into the rabid face of Grizzly. Only it couldn't be Grizzly. The bear-man was one of his best friends. Which meant the shapeshifter had assumed the likeness of the hybrid. He started to draw his Bowies when the creature raised its arms, as if about to unleash its claws.

Forgetting himself, Raphaela dashed in close and blurted, "Grizzly? Is that you? Stop it!"

"Don't interfere!" the man-beast snapped. "I know what I'm doing. This isn't Blade, it's a shapeshifter. We must kill it."

"No," Raphaela said, trying to grab his forearm and missing when he jerked it aside. "This is the real Blade. You mustn't hurt him."

Grizzly backhanded her across the cheek, the blow dropping her dazed to the floor. He looked down at the Warrior and grinned. "Now it's your turn, scumbag. You may have tricked them, but I know what you are." In a flash his fingers stiffened and out popped the five bear claws on each hand.

Blade let go of the knives, realizing the truth. It *was* Grizzly. The shapeshifter possessed the ability to mold itself into a mirror image of any creature it wanted, but so far as he knew, the resemblance was purely superficial, purely an external change. The shapeshifter didn't acquire the internal organs or inherent characteristics of the human or other being it resembled. And since Grizzly's claws were housed in sheaths under his skin, extending from just behind the bear-man's fingernails to above his knobby knuckles, there was no way the shapeshifter could duplicate them.

"Die!" Grizzly roared, about to execute a fierce swipe when a reddish blur rammed into him, bashing him to the floor.

"What the hell has gotten into you?" Jaguarundi demanded, standing astride his fellow hybrid. "Blade isn't the shapeshifter, you idiot."

"Athena told me you would say that," Grizzly replied.

"Athena?" Jag repeated in astonishment, and his momentary shock cost him.

The bear-man came up in a swift spring and brutally kneed the cat-man in the groin, doubling Jag over. He drove his right hand into the side of Jag's neck, using the hard outer edge of his palm instead of his claws, and the cat-man fell. Shifting, Grizzly tensed to jump on the Warrior, but found his adversary already upright.

"The shapeshifter has brainwashed you somehow," Blade stated, his huge fists clenched. "Athena is dead. You should know that."

"She is not!" Grizzly growled. "She's here now."

"Oh?" Blade said. "Don't you remember Death Master?"

Grizzly's brow knit and he blinked a few times. "Death Master?" he repeated. "Why does that name ring a bell?"

"Because he's the son of a bitch who killed Athena," Blade said, gratified to see confusion on the hybrid's face, hoping he could bring Grizzly to his senses and avert an attack. If not, he would be hard-pressed to defeat the man-beast without hurting him.

"Wait a minute!" Grizzly exclaimed. "It's starting to come back to me!"

Blade smiled, a smile that froze on his lips when an enormous shape sprang from behind a stack of boxes situated directly to the hybrid's rear. Blade pointed and opened his mouth to cry a warning.

The creature brought its balled right hand crashing into the top of Grizzly's skull and the bear-man collapsed. It laughed, a raspy, guttural sound, and fixed its alien orbs on the Warrior. "How very clever of you to remind him of her death. It was the one thing that could break the drug's influence. Of course, if I'd had more time to work with him . . ." it said, and let the sentence trail off.

Blade said nothing. At last he was gazing upon the shapeshifter's natural form. The sight chilled him to his marrow.

Zhongli Quan stood over eight feet in height and possessed a decidedly reptilian build. Smooth dark-gray skin lent him an appropriately sinister aspect. His legs were long and thin, his feet having four slender toes much like a lizard's. His five fingers were also thin and bony. A neck the size of a man's wrist served as a perch for an oversized watermelon-shaped head. The eyes were three inches in diameter with eerie red pupils. A mouth six inches wide bristled with razor-tipped teeth.

Whipping the Bowies out, Blade bent at the waist and glared. "Let's finish it, Gualaon. Just you and me."

"My sentiments exactly," Quan stated, stepping over Grizzly's prostrate form. "The Assassins will take care of your friends while I gorge myself on you."

"First you have to kill me."

"That's easily accomplished," Quan said, and lunged with the speed of a striking cobra.

Blade tried to spear the Bowies into the shapeshifter's torso but Zhongli Quan grabbed his wrists, clamping down until it felt as if his skin would burst and holding his arms fast. The creature's maw opened wide, and those horrid teeth were poised to bite into his face. Knowing he couldn't hope to match Quan's might, Blade resorted to finesse, to the deadly skills honed in a hundred violent encounters, automatically striking at one of the creature's weak points.

The Warrior raised his right heel and slammed it onto Quan's left foot, on those slender toes. Something crunched loudly.

Zhongli Quan arched his back and vented a thunderous roar as he let go of the giant's arms and moved backward, limping terribly.

Blade lunged, trying for a killing stroke, both knives surging upward, but he never connected. The shapeshifter recovered incredibly fast, its left hand whipping out and closing on his throat.

"*At last!*" Quan bellowed, and squeezed, his sinews rippling.

Suddenly unable to breathe, Blade felt the thing's fingers digging into his flesh. In another moment his throat would be crushed to a pulp.

Doc Madsen saw the gleaming blade sweeping at his arm. He flinched, expecting his limb to be cut in half the very next instant.

An M-16 chattered.

The edge of the sword was mere inches from the gunfighter's arm when a blistering hail of lead smacked into the man's chest, stitching a line of crimson dots in its wake, and the impact lifted the killer from his face and hurled him rearward over a yard to land with a thud on his back.

Doc glanced around and saw Lobo grinning and wagging the barrel of his rifle.

"Looks like you owe me one, dude."

"Thanks, pardner. I do."

From the front end of the warehouse came the sounds of a commotion. Voices were upraised in anger.

"We must find our friends," Sparrow Hawk declared, taking the lead, his spear held ready for a throw.

Doc fell into step, scouring the stacks and piles. The guy with the crossbow was still up there somewhere.

"Hurry," Sparrow urged them, breaking into a run. "They are in trouble."

"Not so fast, dipstick," Lobo cautioned, trailing behind both of them. "You'll waltz into an ambush. We don't want to get racked ourselves."

But the Flathead paid no attention. He pulled ahead of them, heedless of his safety.

"Wait, dummy!" Lobo called out.

The gunfighter increased his pace, trying to keep an eye on Sparrow and the supplies at the same time. He saw something move near the top of a pile of lumber, something black, and the killer using the crossbow popped up, a shaft set to fire. The hooded figure aimed at Sparrow Hawk.

"Up there!" Lobo shouted.

Doc was already halting and angling the Magnum upward, his left hand rigid and held over the revolver's hammer. Three times he slapped his palm down. Three times he fanned the gun, yet all three shots sounded as one.

At the booming retort the man in black staggered, his body twisting to the left. The crossbow fell from his slack fingers and he clutched feebly at the three new holes in his chest, the holes that were perfectly aligned with his heart. He gurgled, spurting blood from his mouth, and toppled.

The three Force members raced onward.

It was against Blade's nature to succumb without a struggle. He stabbed his left Bowie into Quan's side, sinking the knife all the way to the hilt.

The shapeshifter only laughed. "Keep trying, fool.

Don't deprive me of this precious amusement."

Blade stared up into the creature's malevolent eyes, tensing his shoulders for a try at burying a Bowie in its head. His lungs were in agony, his throat on the verge of splitting. Dizziness assailed him, his vision blurring. In a fleeting panic he swung wildly, but his willpower seemed to have turned to mush. Gritting his teeth, he shook his head and tried to jerk loose.

Zhongli Quan grunted and shuddered violently, his hand slipping from the Warrior's neck.

Tottering to one side, Blade gulped in air and raised the Bowies defensively in anticipation of being torn apart at any moment. His eyesight cleared and he gazed in astonishment at his nemesis.

A heavy spear had penetrated the shapeshifter's head from behind, bored completely through its skull, and burst out between its fiery orbs. Quan's hands gripped the gore-coated front of the shaft, his mouth opening and closing much like that of a fish out of water. He tugged, succeeding in drawing the spear a few inches forward.

Blade realized the creature was trying to extract the Flathead lance. He didn't know if it could heal itself after sustaining such a mortal wound, and he wasn't about to stand around and wait to find out. Taking two strides, he vaulted at Quan's head, his massive arms slashing inward with both Bowies in a crisscrossing pattern.

The big knives bit deep into the shapeshifter's narrow neck, their keen edges, propelled by sinews of iron, slicing the throat nearly in half.

Zhongli screeched as his head flopped to the right, stretching the several inches of neck tissue still intact.

The Warrior alighted and jumped again, his triumphant eyes focused on the shapeshifter's as he repeated the twin strokes. The Bowies severed the neck completely.

With a pronounced plop Zhongli Quan's oversized head

fell to the floor and rolled a few feet before coming to a rest upside down, the spear still jutting from both ends.

As Blade dropped he drove his right leg outward, connecting with the thing's chest, watching blood spray from its stump of a neck as the enormous body slowly fell backwards. The creature slammed onto the concrete, the arms outstretched, and quivered a bit before stiffening.

"Not bad, dude. I couldn't have done better myself."

His throat in torment, Blade glanced around to find Lobo, Doc Madsen, and Sparrow Hawk ten yards away. He wiped his Bowies clean on his pants, then stepped to the shapeshifter's head. Placing his right combat boot on top to hold the ghastly cranium steady, he took hold of the end of the spear and wrenched. With a protracted sucking sound the spear slid out.

"Yuck. Talk about gross," Lobo commented.

Blade walked over to the Flathead and extended the weapon. "I believe this is yours," he croaked.

"I was wondering what had happened to it," Sparrow stated with a smile.

"Hey, Blade," Lobo said.

"What?"

"Have you ever played kickball?"

The Warrior looked at the Clansman. "Kickball?"

"Yeah. It's a game my old gang used to play back in the Twin Cities," Lobo explained. "It's a lot of fun."

"Why in the world are you mentioning it now?"

"Oh, no special reason," Lobo said, and before anyone could stop him he dashed up to Zhongli Quan's head and booted it halfway to the entrance.

EPILOGUE

Blade sat at his desk in the command bunker at the Force Facility, deep in thought. Governor Melnick would arrive at any minute and he must give a verbal report on everything that had transpired since his return from Mesaville. He didn't know how the governor would take the news about General Gallagher, nor the revelation that there might be more shapeshifters occupying positions of authority in California.

He heard someone enter the upstairs door and waited as they hurried down the steps and knocked.

"It's open."

In came Raphaela, her features pale, her expression one of shock. She walked to his desk and mechanically saluted.

Blade leaned on the desk. "What's wrong? Is Governor Melnick here?"

"Nope," Raphaela replied, and cleared her throat.

"Then what's the matter? You look as if you've seen a ghost."

"I have."

"Are you going to keep me in suspense or is this a secret we both can share?"

VENGEANCE STRIKE

The Molewoman recovered her composure and grinned. "There's someone here to see you."

"I don't have an appointment with anyone other than the governor."

"Oh, I think you'll want to see this guy."

"Why? Who is it?"

"Someone who wants to join the Force. He just showed up at the front gate and Jag and Grizzly escorted him to the bunkers."

"They should know better. I don't take in new recruits off the street."

"You might make an exception this time."

Annoyed by her stalling, Blade rose and said, "Who the heck is it?"

Raphaela beamed and unloaded her bombshell. "A staff sergeant in Special Forces. He says his name is Stephen Havoc."